SHADOW OF CLORINDA

SHADOW OF CLORINDA

Katrina Wright

CHIVERS

British Library Cataloguing in Publication Data available

This Large Print edition published by AudioGO Ltd, Bath, 2013.
Published by arrangement with the Author.

U.K. Hardcover   ISBN   978 1 4713 2023 1
U.K. Softcover   ISBN   978 1 4713 2024 8

Printed and bound in Great Britain by
MPG Books Group Limited

CHAPTER ONE

Kitty peered anxiously out of the coach as it came to a sudden, jolting stop.

Surely they had not reached Fallows yet? There were no lights, only the carriage lamps like fireflies in the gathering dark, and bleak moorland rising on either side; with a clump of trees to her right, just visible.

'Why have you stopped?' she called to the coachman, trying to keep the tremor out of her voice.

His gruff tones came back to her. 'There's a woman here, my lady, standing in the road.'

Kitty leaned further out and caught a glimpse of a figure in black, a hood pulled up over her head and a basket on her arm.

'Who are you? What do you want?' she demanded imperiously.

The woman moved round to stand beside the window and look up at her, though Kitty could not see her face clearly as it was hidden by the cloak and hood.

'White heather for luck, me lady?' a voice whined. 'Take it and the luck of the gipsies will be with ye.'

'No thank you,' Kitty said haughtily. 'Drive on, coachman.'

'Ye'll be needing it, ma'am,' the rough voice hissed in her ear. 'Take it, and I'll tell ye something meant for Sir Rupert's bride alone. Here.' She held out a bunch of white heather and, unwillingly, Kitty took it in her gloved hand.

The dark face was pushed nearer to hers. 'Beware of Clorinda,' the woman whispered, and Kitty felt a sudden icy chill tingle up her spine. Clorinda was the name of Rupert's first wife—but Clorinda was dead.

'What do you mean?' she faltered. 'My fiance's first wife is no more—she has passed away, two years since.'

'Beware of Clorinda,' the woman repeated, and then, in the darkness, like a vision that had not been real, she was gone; and only the wind howled mournfully across the bleak moorland.

The coachman whipped up the horses, and Kitty sank back against the plush seat, gazing uneasily at the few sprigs of white heather in her hand. Who had the woman been? Why had she felt it necessary to warn her against a dead person? What could Clorinda do? She had been laid in her grave, and Rupert had no mistress now to glide through the rooms of Fallows and stand at his side when welcoming guests. Except that soon, in six weeks, she, Lady Katherine Mallory, would be his new bride to take Clorinda's place.

The coach turned in through high pillars, even as she pondered on the strange encounter with the gipsy woman, and the coachman called reassuringly, 'Here we be, my lady.

Fallows at last. You're home.'

Home! Yes, this was to be her new home, and she could see that she was welcomed and awaited. Lights blazed from the windows and, as she was assisted from the coach, the tall, dark figure of her future husband—which always made her heart leap ever since she had first seen him at the ball in London six months ago—came striding down the steps from the great door to sweep her unceremoniously into his arms.

'Kitty! At last!'

'Oh, Rupert,' she whispered tremulously, her senses in a turmoil at his nearness.

'You're more beautiful than ever,' he told her ardently. 'How was your journey? Are you exhausted? What do you think of Yorkshire?'

She laughed with happiness. 'One question at a time, please. The journey was very comfortable, thanks to your care and forethought. And I am not exhausted, but thrilled to be here. So far, however, I have not made up my mind about Yorkshire. It is certainly different from London.'

'You'll soon grow to love it, as I do,' he told her, as helped her up the steps, and into a hall where there was warmth and cheer. 'Come, love, Mrs Potter will take you to the room which you are to occupy until the wedding, and then you shall have something to eat and drink.' Suddenly he noticed the little bunch of white heather in her hand. 'Why, what's this?'

'Oh, Rupert, it was ever so odd,' Kitty told him, her fears banished now in the security of his presence and the light of the lamps. 'Just before we arrived here, a strange woman stopped the coach, and gave me this heather. She said it would bring me the luck of the gipsies, and that I would need it.' She frowned. 'She also told me to—but, no, it was nonsense. Not worth bothering your ears with.'

He spoke gravely. 'No gipsies—and none have been given permission to camp upon my land—have the right to waylay you with threats that if you don't take their lucky charms and pay them, you'll be cursed. Tell me what she said, sweetheart.'

'She didn't ask for any money, or threaten me with a curse,' Kitty said, slowly. She looked up at him. 'All she would say was "Beware of Clorinda".'

He shook his head. 'Well, we have some odd characters wandering the moor, but this is ridiculous. It didn't disturb you, did it, love?'

She hesitated. 'No, not really, but Clorinda really is dead, isn't she, Rupert? She can't hurt me?'

'I was at her bedside when she died; she had the child she gave her life to bear—vainly, for it too was born dead,' Rupert said heavily, his voice and eyes dark with painful recollection. 'She was not turned seventeen, Kitty, but I can show you their joint resting-place—hers and that of my dead daughter, who never drew the

4

breath of life.'

Kitty was stricken with remorse. She put her hand upon his arm. 'I'm sorry, Rupert. I should not have troubled you with foolish fears and the prattling of an old woman. I know it must even now be distressing for you to think of Clorinda's death.'

He looked into her eyes as he spoke, and she could not doubt his sincerity. 'The match was to please my father, who was on his deathbed. I was fond of Clorinda but I did not love her as I love you. The tragedy was that she died so young, having known so little of life and its happiness. She was a sweet and gentle child. I would never have wished her harm, even though my father died soon after we were married, and I had to resign myself to a marriage where true love—love such as I have for you—had no place.'

He paused, then went on in a different tone, 'But enough of past troubles. We must look to the future. Clorinda lies at rest, and you are going to be as happy as I can make you here at Fallows.'

He turned and called for the housekeeper, who had been standing discreetly out of earshot. When she came forward, Rupert said, 'This is Mrs Potter, who will show you your room. Mrs Potter, Lady Katherine will be your new mistress when our wedding takes place in six weeks' time, so treat her with all due respect and obedience.' He grinned at

Kitty. 'Mrs Potter is the mainstay of Fallows, my darling. She wields the power of the keys in the kitchen—and over all of us, too.'

Kitty held out her hand to the housekeeper, in her neat black with its touches of white at neck and wrists. Mrs Potter gave a dignified little curtsey as she said, 'Welcome to Fallows, my lady.'

'Thank you. I hope we'll be friends, and you need not worry that I shall interfere with your running of the house,' Kitty replied.

She looked round. The hall and the rooms that she could see leading off it were spotless and comfortable, and there was a fresh scent of cleanliness, the homely smells of beeswax, lavender and polish everywhere. Mrs Potter was obviously an excellent housekeeper.

'Go to your room, now, and take off your cloak, darling, and then Mrs Potter will bring you down for refreshment,' Rupert urged, and obediently, Kitty mounted the stairs with their shining, old, wooden treads in the wake of the stately housekeeper.

After traversing a confusing number of passages, she was shown into a room which had the same charm and comfort as the rest of the house. Soft green draperies screened the window, and matched the cover and canopy of the large four-poster bed. The wash-stand and furniture too echoed the same green motif, though Kitty was enchanted to see, as Mrs Potter lit the lamp from the candle she carried, that there were several pieces which were obviously very old, their dark wood shining with polish and elbow-grease.

'Why, this is delightful, Mrs Potter,' she exclaimed impulsively.

'We call it the Green Room, my lady—the reason's obvious,' the housekeeper replied, with the trace of a smile. 'It is one of the best guest rooms. You will naturally be moving into the master suite after the marriage, but I hope you will be comfortable here until then.'

'I'm sure I shall,' Kitty said, warmly, and stopped suddenly, as she caught the fragrance of an unfamiliar perfume, just a whiff at first, and then strengthening until the room was full of it. 'What is that scent?' she asked, wondering where the perfume had come from. 'It's beautiful. Like—like a garden full of spring flowers after rain.'

'Scent?' Mrs Potter echoed, obviously puzzled. 'I can smell nothing, my lady, except perhaps the herbs where we lay the linen. Maybe that's what you can smell, the herbs from the linen-room.'

'No—no, this is very strong. Why, it's almost as if a perfume bottle had been overturned. I shall have to open the window,' Kitty said, stepping across to the green draperies, and throwing open one of the small, diamond-paned windows.

Her room was situated in the oldest part of the house, obviously. Rupert had told her that

7

the central section went back to the time of the Tudors, though it had been much altered and rebuilt and added to since then.

A cool breeze began to waft the scent of the perfume out through the window, and Kitty turned to Mrs Potter.

'Did the late mistress have any special scent?' she asked slowly, and Mrs Potter turned away to straighten the soft towels that lay on the wash-stand.

'Well, my lady, I wasn't her maid, but I do know that she loved flowers, and to please her, the master went to some foreign place—Paris, I think it was—and there was a perfume made that was sold to nobody else. It was called "Clorinda" after her, you see.'

'Is there any left in the house?' Kitty demanded, and the housekeeper made a gesture with her hand.

'I don't know, my lady. All her things were stored in one of the trunks upstairs in the attics, and nobody goes there. I suppose there might have been some scent amongst her gowns.'

There and then, Kitty made up her mind to go and find out whether the perfume that only she seemed to be able to smell had been Clorinda's. Tomorrow, she would go up to the attics, and look through her predecessor's trunks. But now, she recollected guiltily, Rupert was awaiting her downstairs, and she hastily took off her cloak and bonnet, splashed her hands and face at the wash-stand where hot water had been brought for her arrival, and smoothed her hair.

'Thank you, Mrs Potter, you may show me the room where Sir Rupert is waiting for me,' she said, lifting her head haughtily. It would never do for the housekeeper to suspect that she was feeling more than a little disturbed by the happenings of the last few hours; first the gipsy and now the scent.

'Yes, my lady. You did not bring a maid? Then I will assign Lucy to perform that duty until you can choose a maid of your own. I think you will find her willing and biddable,' Mrs. Potter, told her, picking up her candle once more, and blowing out the lamp.

The cool breeze was still coming in through the window, and the scent had almost disappeared. Almost—but not quite, and Kitty tried to imprint it on her memory so that she would not forget it, before she followed the housekeeper from the room.

*   *   *

Downstairs, with the tall figure of Rupert at her side, fortified with good food and wine, and with the soft glow of the lamps dispelling her feelings of uneasiness, Kitty relaxed and enjoyed the pleasure of simply being with her beloved.

They had met in London and had fallen in

love within only a few weeks of their meeting. He had told her the full story of his previous marriage, and how it had ended in tragedy, but had assured her that what he felt for her was completely different from the love he had entertained for his first wife.

Kitty indeed had wondered whether she would find it difficult to fit into the role of a second wife but her doubts were dispelled completely as they came to know each other. So, when Rupert suggested that they should set their marriage date for July, and that he would go on ahead to prepare the house in Yorkshire for her, she had agreed eagerly.

There had been no opposition from her Mama, who saw Rupert as the catch of the season. His suggestion that she came to Fallows a few weeks before her wedding to familiarise herself with her new home and get to know the people she would be living among, pleased Kitty, who felt that it would give her a little time to catch her breath before actually embarking upon the strange seas of marriage.

Her father was dead but her mama planned to come north to attend the ceremony, for Rupert had insisted that, as she was marrying into an old and noble family, Kitty's wedding should take place at the ancient church in the village near Fallows, where all the Hamill men before him had married their wives.

Kitty was pleased again, for she did not want the trappings of a big, society wedding in

London, and she had brought her trousseau with her, including the veil and wedding gown of heavy, cream, corded silk, with its delicate trimmings of lace and seed pearls.

That evening, as Rupert showed her a few of the downstairs rooms by lamplight, she realised just how much she had missed him in the few days they had been apart. He was telling her the story of one of his ancestors, whose painting hung on the wall, when suddenly he stopped and said, with mock severity, 'I fear I am wasting my breath. I am sure you are not listening to Sir Humphrey's adventures.'

He looked down at her expectantly.

'No,' Kitty admitted, and dimpled. 'I was just looking at you. Oh, my darling, how I have missed you.'

'And I you,' he replied. Then he swore, 'Damn! I cannot even kiss you here in case one of the servants should see us. Oh, why did I suggest we waited six weeks to be married?'

Kitty felt her limbs turn to water at the expression in his blue eyes.

'Just wait until our honeymoon, my love,' he breathed. 'You with that corn-coloured hair loose round your shoulders—and just the two of us, alone . . .'

Kitty blushed, and he put an arm fiercely round her, saying, 'Let us proceed with our little tour, or I'll be tempted to sweep you off upstairs to my room, wedded or not.' He led her through a door. 'This is the Winter Parlour.'

The room was cosy, done out in autumn colours, but Kitty's eyes went straight to the portrait that hung over the fireplace. Even in the light of the lamp that Rupert carried, she could see that the girl who smiled from the frame was beautiful. She was simply dressed as a shepherdess, carrying a little crook decorated with a ribbon, and her copper hair flew in the wind.

'What a lovely girl!' Kitty exclaimed. 'Was she also one of your ancestors?'

'No, darling. That is—was—Clorinda,' Rupert said, his expression changing. 'It is the only portrait of her that I have left hanging in the house, out of deference to your feeling, but I did not think you would be hurt if I left it. Even down to the colour of her hair, she seems to belong in this room.'

Kitty nodded slowly. Such a beautiful girl, so full of youth and the joy of living, and yet she had died before she was seventeen. Could she grudge Clorinda one small memory in this house where she had been the mistress for so short a time?

'No, let her be,' she said impulsively. 'She should have a place here, for after all, she was Lady Hamill, and she almost bore you a daughter.'

'My generous girl! I knew you would feel that way,' Rupert told her, holding her

12

against his shoulder, as they both looked up at Clorinda's innocent sweetness, the slender form, and the amber eyes smiling down at them.

Just then, the great grandfather clock in the hall whirred ponderously, and struck the hour.

'Why it's midnight,' Kitty said, as the chimes faded away. 'I should have been in bed long since, but I had forgotten the time in my delight at being reunited with you once more, Rupert. But I am weary after my journey and now I really must retire, for otherwise I will be too tired to get up tomorrow.'

'I'll take you to the door of your room until you learn the way yourself,' he said, and led her up the stairs and along the shadowy corridors. Outside her door, he kissed her lightly, but with restrained passion.

'Goodnight, my darling. Sleep well.'

'Goodnight, Rupert,' Kitty answered, and entered her room.

CHAPTER TWO

A figure, dozing in the big chair, started up as the door opened. Kitty saw that the lamp was lit, the bed turned back ready for her to retire, and a nightgown laid out for her. The window had been shut, and the green draperies fell smoothly at the far side of the room.

Curtseying before her was a small maid in cap and apron.

'I'm Lucy, my lady,' announced the child; she was hardly more than twelve or thirteen. 'I'm to be your maid, if you please.'

'Well, that is a pleasant surprise. But you should not have stayed up so late, Lucy,' Kitty said.

'Mrs Potter said I must wait for you, to see if you needed me,' the girl replied. 'I'll bring your hot water now, and help you undress.'

She went to the door, and it creaked softly behind her, while Kitty wandered to the table where all her toiletries had been carefully laid out. Sitting before the mirror, she began to take the pins slowly from her hair. Then suddenly, she stopped, her hand arrested in mid-air. Her own perfume bottle was there, but there was another, unfamiliar one standing next to it.

Kitty felt her heart begin to pound. The bottle was beautifully shaped in pale green. The label upon it proclaimed the name of a famous Parisian perfumier and, beneath, the word "Clorinda." Kitty lifted the bottle with trembling fingers, and pulled the stopper. The same fresh fragrance that had filled the room earlier on came to her nostrils, though the bottle was empty but for a few dregs in the bottom.

While she was sitting, still wondering what this meant, Lucy returned with her hot water,

14

and Kitty spun round on the stool.

'Did you put this here, Lucy?' she demanded, holding out the green bottle and the girl shook her head bewilderedly.

'No my lady. I unpacked your boxes, and hung your gowns in the closet, and laid your linen away in the tallboy, and put out your things as you can see. But that bottle—I never put it there, I swear.'

'But you have been in the room all the time, watching for me to come to bed, have you not?' Kitty asked, and the girl flushed.

'Yes, my lady, but—I am afraid I fell asleep for a while.'

'Then while you were asleep, someone else could have crept in and placed this with my own things,' Kitty said thoughtfully.

'I suppose they could have, my lady, but they would have had to be very quiet,' Lucy said wonderingly. She stared. 'It's the mistress—I mean, the late mistress's perfume, isn't it?'

'Yes it is. And earlier on today, soon after I arrived, the whole room was full of the same scent, though Mrs Potter said she could smell nothing. Can you smell the scent in this bottle?' Kitty asked, holding it out, and Lucy took a sniff, and nodded.

'Yes, of course, my lady. She always wore it. It was specially made for her.'

'Lucy, I'm baffled,' Kitty declared frankly. 'Why fill my room with Clorinda's perfume? And why couldn't Mrs Potter smell it earlier

15

on? Is there one of the servants, or the staff who resents my coming? Anyone who was devoted to your late mistress, for instance? Her own maid, perhaps?'

Lucy pondered, her freckled face screwed up in thought. Then she said, 'No, my lady, speaking for myself, like, I'm thrilled to be chosen to attend to your wants, and everyone below stairs is pleased that the house will have a new mistress. We've all been saying—' She went red suddenly. 'Well, we do talk, you know, and everybody's been saying how lovely and ladylike you are, and how kind and sweet-looking, and what a lovely bride you'll be. As for Lady Clorinda's maid, she never had one, only a girl from the village, who was training to be a lady's maid, that she brought with her when she married, and after she died, Betty went off to work for some fine lady in London. There's nobody here wishes you ill, ma'am, that I'll swear.'

Kitty shrugged. 'I see. Well, thank you, Lucy.' She smiled at the girl. 'I hope we'll get along well together. I'm not a hard mistress to please, and I'd far rather have you than some French lady's maid with her nose stuck up in the air. Thank you for doing my unpacking. But you must be tired. You go off to bed now, and I'll undress myself. Oh, and about the bottle. Don't say anything to any of the others, will you? It's very strange, and I don't want to start gossip.'

'I won't breathe a word, my lady,' Lucy vowed, and added impulsively, 'I hope everything goes well for you, my lady. I hope you'll be happy here.'

*   *   *

The following evening, Rupert had invited two or three of his oldest friends to a small dinner party to welcome Kitty to Fallows. He spent the day showing her the house and grounds, and the cobwebs of the night cleared in the fresh air that swept warmly across the open moorland.

Even the affair of the perfume bottle seemed to fade into insignificance. After all, why shouldn't someone have wanted to make her a present of the very expensive scent that Clorinda had used? She had been foolish to read any more into it than that, she decided.

She was a little apprehensive about the dinner party, however, though Rupert assured her there was no need to be.

'They are people I grew up with, and they'll love you as I do,' he told her, as they strolled in the old-fashioned walled garden behind the house. 'Rosalind and Sebastian Meade have been my friends since childhood—they are brother and sister, the son and daughter of Rowland Meade, who settled here and made a fortune from his woollen mills. Their house is not very far from Fallows. Look, on that hilltop over there, where there is a clump of trees. The house is on the other side.'

Kitty looked, and smiled to herself at Rupert calling the slight ridge a hilltop. The Meade house appeared to be about a mile away.

'And who else is coming?' she asked, taking his arm.

'The Vicar, who will conduct our wedding, and the local doctor,' he told her. 'The Vicar is a sweet, charming person, it would be impossible to dislike him, and Edward— Doctor Parsons—has become a friend since he came to practise here. He attended Clorinda during her illness.'

'Illness? I thought she died in childbirth,' Kitty said, frowning.

Rupert lowered his head. 'She was very delicate,' he confided. 'During the last month, she had to keep to her bed. It was something to do with her having to rest as much as possible. Edward was here constantly.'

There was pain in his voice, and Kitty said no more, since she saw no reason to stir up unhappy memories. Instead, she turned the conversation to the flowers, which were a profusion of sweet-smelling colour, and Rupert lost the lines of tension about his eyes.

Smiling now, he took her hand and kissed it ardently, and they walked on, enjoying the sunshine and each other's company, blissfully happy . . .

18

The blissful mood continued until Kitty was preparing for dinner that evening. She had chosen a cream-coloured gown which emphasised her fair colouring, and Lucy had laid it out on the bed together with her gloves and fan, and the crisply starched petticoats that pushed out the skirt.

While she sat in the hip bath surrounded by scented water, and dried herself on the soft towels, Kitty debated idly whether to wear her diamond earrings or her sapphires, which brought out the blue of her eyes, which were almost grey-green at times, in contrast to Rupert's clear blue gaze.

Lucy helped her to dress as the other maids scurried away with the water from her bath, and when she emerged from behind the screen, and surveyed herself in the long mirror, she had to admit she was satisfied with her toilette. Now for her hair, jewels and gloves.

But even as she sat for Lucy to brush out her long hair and twine it into a more ladylike style high on her head, something caught her eyes, and she turned. The gloves that went with the gown were of soft cream, but the gloves that were lying on the bed were not the right ones.

'Lucy, my gloves,' Kitty said bewilderedly. 'Bring them here, if you please.'

The girl picked them up, and exclaimed, 'but my lady, these are not the ones I laid out

19

for you.'

She handed them to Kitty, who drew one over her fingers. It was far too small for her, and did not fit.

'Whose gloves are these?' Kitty demanded. 'They are certainly not mine.'

Her gaze met Lucy's, and the girl looked frightened. 'They are a lady's gloves, ma'am. None of the servants possess gloves like that.'

Again their eyes met, but Kitty did not even have to ask the question that sprang to her mind. Lucy said reluctantly, 'The late mistress—had very tiny hands, ma'am.'

'Clorinda, again,' Kitty breathed, and she pushed the gloves at Lucy. 'Take them away,' she ordered, trying to keep the rising panic from her voice, and as Lucy fled from the room, Kitty's hand went to her throat. She found she was trembling. First the perfume, now the gloves. Everywhere she turned, she seemed to find Clorinda. What did it mean? Who was doing this to her? And most important of all—why?

*   *   *

Kitty dismissed Lucy and said she would do her own hair. Though she had been brought up in the lap of luxury, she did not believe in never being able to manage for herself, which was why she had brought no maid with her. And, shaken by the episode of Clorinda's

20

gloves mysteriously appearing in place of her own, she did not want Lucy to see how disturbed she was.

When the girl had gone, she quickly twisted her hair, which curled naturally, up on top of her head, and secured it with pins, adding a diamond clip. She decided against the earrings, and put on only a matching bracelet over the gloves which she took from her glove drawer. A dab of her own perfume on her handkerchief, and she was ready—cool and beautiful, as her mirror told her, with her slender shoulders revealed by the low neck of the gown.

She took a deep breath. Shaken as she was, she must face the guests with no indication that anything was wrong, and she picked up her fan and glided from the room, leaving the lamp burning. Somehow, she did not want to put it out.

As she closed the door of her room behind her, she almost collided with a figure hurrying past. It was Mrs Potter, immaculate as always, who immediately drew back to let Kitty precede her to the head of the stairs. But Kitty stopped, puzzled. The far end of the corridor led, so Rupert had told her, only to a few store-rooms, so what had the housekeeper been doing there when she was just about to serve up dinner for guests?

'I'm sorry, my lady,' Mrs Potter said, bobbing a curtsey. 'May I add that you look very lovely tonight?'

The housekeeper folded her hands. In the light of the lamps that lit the passage, her eyes were cast down, her face inscrutable.

'I have my duties to attend to, ma'am,' she replied calmly.

'But there are only store-rooms down there, aren't there?' Kitty asked.

The housekeeper agreed, 'yes, my lady. Only store-rooms.'

Kitty was about to question her further, when she remembered that she was not yet the mistress of the house, and perhaps there had been some reason why Mrs Potter had had to visit the store-rooms. But then, as she turned away, she noticed the housekeeper slip a key into her pocket with a gesture that was distinctly furtive.

Troubled, she walked to the head of the stairs, deciding that tomorrow, she would explore the store-room. The housekeeper appeared innocent enough, but there had been the incident where she had sworn she could not smell Clorinda's perfume, even though it filled the room. Had she been lying? Had it been her, even, who had tipped up the bottle on to the carpet while Kitty was not looking? For the young woman recalled that the scent had sprung suddenly from nowhere, and that the bottle she had found afterwards had been almost empty.

Convinced that there was something

suspicious about the housekeeper, she walked thoughtfully down the stairs, and was swept up by Rupert's admiration, and the strange faces of the guests who were waiting for her. Introductions were made.

Rosalind Meade, a tawny-haired, green-eyed beauty, smiled and declared, 'I want us to become very dear friends, Lady Katherine—'

'Oh, please, won't you call me Kitty, as Rupert does?' the young woman invited, charmed by Rosalind's bubbling personality. She too hoped they would become friends. It would be pleasant to have a friend and confidante like this lively, impulsive creature.

'Rupert is a very fortunate man,' Sebastian Meade said, bowing over her hand, and holding it for longer than was necessary. The admiration in the green eyes that were like his sister's made Kitty blush, for Sebastian was by no means unattractive. He was tall and fair, and he shared Rosalind's charm. 'In fact,' he declared, 'I might have challenged him in the lists for your favour if he had not been engaged to marry you so shortly. But be warned my lady, I will not give up easily. I might persuade you to elope with me on the night before your wedding.'

'At your peril, Sebastian,' Rupert cried, his eyes openly adoring Kitty. 'She is mine.'

The Vicar, a slightly stooped figure in clerical black, intervened tactfully. 'I can see that Lady Katherine will make a charming bride. May I wish you every happiness, ma'am,' he intoned, looking at Kitty benignly. 'And many long years as mistress of Fallows.'

'I second that.' It was the young doctor, Edward Parsons, who spoke. 'The house needs a mistress again, and you seem to bring a breath of spring to these dark rooms, Lady Katherine. Please accept my sincere congratulations. I can see that you will make Rupert very happy, and as his friend, I am delighted by his good fortune at winning such a lovely wife.'

Kitty turned from one to another with a smile. 'I don't know what to say.' She laughed. 'You are all so kind—I feel that I shall never be anything but happy if I am accepted by the people around as you have accepted me.'

Just then, Robbs, the butler, announced that dinner was served, and a move was made towards the dining-room. Kitty found herself on Sebastian's arm, while Rupert led in Rosalind. The young man leaned over towards her.

'I meant what I said, you know,' he murmured passionately. 'You're the loveliest thing I have ever seen, and I have fallen madly in love with you. If I can take you from Rupert, I shall. After all, they say all is fair in love and war.'

Kitty decided to treat this lightly. 'I'll warrant I am not the first young lady you've fallen madly in love with, Mr Meade. But

I can see that you don't believe in wasting words.' She smiled, tapping him with her fan, and then any reply he might have wished to make was lost as they seated themselves at the huge, old refectory table. But Kitty was slightly worried. She did hope that she would not have to be rude to one of Rupert's oldest friends, but if Sebastian continued to make himself a nuisance, she could see no other way of getting rid of him.

*   *   *

The dinner party was a great success and when, after playing the piano and singing together, the evening came to an end, Kitty was tired, but blushingly happy as their guests said goodnight.

'We must see a great deal of each other, Kitty,' Rosalind declared, holding Kitty's hand as she stood in the hall in her cloak and bonnet. 'I'll ride over to visit you. When? Tomorrow?'

'Whenever you like.' Kitty laughed, charmed by her new friend's impetuosity.

'Perhaps you'll come riding with me, and I can show you the moors while Rupert is busy. He will have to be busy at least some of the time before you are married,' Rosalind said sweepingly. 'He can't monopolise you all the hours of every day.'

'And I too will see you again, Lady

Katherine,' Sebastian's smooth voice announced, and his hand tightened round her fingers as he bent to kiss them. She wanted to snatch her arm away, but did not dare, and had to submit to his touch, though she felt he was being unfair to Rupert.

After everyone had gone, her betrothed led the way back into the drawing-room for a cup of cocoa which Mrs Potter had waiting, and they sat by the window, enjoying the cool evening air—for the night was sultry—and sipping their drinks.

'How homely this is,' Rupert suddenly remarked, leaning back and stretching out his long legs. 'An evening with friends—but it's even more pleasant when the evening comcs to an end and we can just sit and talk over events. We'll have many such evenings in the future, my darling.' His blue eyes were tender as they rested on hers.

Then she said impulsively, 'Is your friend Sebastian always like—well, like he was with me when you have lady guests?'

'He's a flirt,' Rupert said carelessly.

'He told me he was madly in love with me, and would take me away from you if he could,' Kitty confided, and was unprepared for the sudden grimness that settled round Rupert's mouth.

'Sometimes even a friend can go too far.'

'Oh, I took no notice, of course. I pretended to treat it as a joke,' Kitty assured him hastily, and he took her hand and looked deeply into her eyes.

'You're really mine, aren't you, Kitty? No other man will ever come between us?' he demanded, with a violence she had never seen before.

'You know it, Rupert. I love only you. I shall never love anyone else,' she answered, slightly frightened.

'I think—I think I would kill him. Or perhaps kill you,' he said, in a low voice.

Kitty attempted a little laugh which did not quite ring true. 'Why, Rupert, what are you saying? You make me afraid when you talk like that.'

'Forgive me, darling, but I care so much. I couldn't live without you, now that I have found you.'

'Of course I forgive you,' Kitty answered readily, and in a moment, she was in his arms, and he was holding her against his breast and kissing her, so that her senses reeled.

CHAPTER THREE

The next morning, Kitty was awake before Lucy came with the morning tea, in spite of the fact that she had had a late evening. There was something she wanted to do and she determined to do it before the rest of the house was astir.

She slipped out of bed, shrugged on her robe, and slid her feet into mules, then went to the door. It was already light, and she had pulled the curtains a little, so she needed no lamp or candle.

She opened the door, and peered out. As she had expected, the corridor was empty, and the only sounds that she could hear were muted ones from the kitchen quarters, drifting up to her window.

She walked along the corridor in the direction that Mrs Potter had come the previous evening, opening any doors she came to, and glancing into the rooms. As Rupert had told her, they were merely store-rooms, and two of them took her to the end of the corridor. She turned the corner, and came to a full stop. A stout, wooden door faced her, and when she turned the handle it was locked, or appeared to be. She pushed, and after a moment, the door gave way, revealing a flight of stairs.

Kitty could see that they were seldom used, and the paint and paper on the walls was old and peeling. Lifting her robe so as not to soil it in the dust that lay on the stairs, she began to ascend, very cautiously, noticing as she did so that someone did use the stairs, for up the centre of the steps, a swathe of dust had been removed, and there was an odd footmark or two in the dust at the sides.

It was quite dark on the stairs, and Kitty felt a sense of uneasiness come over her. Was this where Mrs Potter had come from the previous evening? What had she been doing in this obviously neglected part of the house? Then she saw, in the dimness, that she had reached a landing, and that three doors opened off it.

She stood still and listened. There was no sound at all, but when she hesitantly tried the door handles, she found that all three were firmly locked, and not just stiff to open.

Puzzled, she stood in the semi-dark, wondering what lay behind the doors. More store rooms? but then, what had Mrs Potter been doing here the previous evening? And which lock was the one that the key she had slipped into her pocket fitted? Kitty resolved to solve the mystery as soon as possible and made her way back down the stairs, shutting the great door at the bottom firmly behind her, before returning to her room. She was back in bed, as though she had just woken, when Lucy came cheerfully in with her tea.

'Oh Lucy,' Kitty said casually, as the girl laid out the dress her mistress intended to wear that day. 'What's at the end of this corridor?'

The girl looked up curiously. 'There are some rooms where old furniture is stored, ma'am, and then a door. I don't know where it leads. It's always been locked as long as I've been here. Nobody ever goes there. Somebody did tell me once that the rooms beyond are not safe, so that's why the door is always locked.'

Well, the door hadn't been locked that morning, Kitty thought to herself, as she sipped her tea.

*   *   *

'Now my darling, what would you like to do today?' Rupert asked, smiling at her as they finished their breakfast. 'I shall need a few hours with the bailiff at some time, but the rest of my day is at your disposal.'

'Well, I've become more and more fascinated with the house, Kitty said artlessly. 'Especially the old part, where my room is. There's a most intriguing door just along the corridor, and I want to know where it leads to.'

'Oh, the Monk's Door? That came from a monastery during the Dissolution, I believe, and the staircase behind it,' Rupert answered casually.

Kitty clasped her hands in genuine delight. 'A Monk's Door? Rupert, why did you never tell me there was such a fascinating feature of the house?'

'Because, my darling, I'm sorry to disappoint you, but the Monk's Stairs lead only to a few rooms which are very poky and never used. The whole of that portion is so old it's regarded as unsafe, so we keep the door locked always, for fear anyone should go wandering about there and meet with an

30

accident,' Rupert told her, and Kitty opened wide, innocent eyes.

'But the door was not locked this morning, Rupert. I managed to push it open.'

'You didn't go up the stairs, did you?' he demanded, frowning, and she decided to play safe with a little white lie.

'Oh no, it looked too dark and musty. But Rupert, I must have the Monk's Door and the Monk's Stairs renovated. I have plenty of money of my own, as you know. I shall make it my very special project,' Kitty told him, and his frown deepened.

'The door should have been locked. I can't imagine how it came to be open. I've never known it open. I even thought the key had been lost, but I suppose Mrs Potter has one—though heaven knows why she should have opened the door,' he said. 'It must be locked again at once. One of the maids might go up the stairs, and I believe there is rot in the boards.' He rang the bell, and summoned the housekeeper. When she came, he said coldly, 'Mrs Potter, who gave you permission to unlock the Monk's Door? You know the place is unsafe.'

The woman turned a puzzled gaze at him. 'The door has not been unlocked, sir. I do not even know where the key is.'

'But I opened it this morning,' Kitty put in impetuously.

Mrs Potter's eyes swivelled round to regard

31

her with a disbelieving look. 'I'm afraid you must have imagined it, my lady.'

'No, I didn't—' Kitty began heatedly.

'There is only one way to settle this,' Rupert interrupted. 'We'll go up there and have a look, now.'

The three of them trooped up the stairs and along the corridor to Kitty's room, past it, and round the corner to the door. It was shut, as Kitty had left it, and when Rupert tried the handle, he could not move the heavy wood.

'I'm sorry, Mrs Potter,' he said, rubbing his hands. 'My fiancee told me she opened the door this morning, but as you say, she probably dreamed it.'

'That would certainly appear to be the explanation. The door has never been opened for years,' the housekeeper added calmly.

Kitty was not satisfied. She said nothing but she knew it hadn't been a dream. Once again, Mrs Potter appeared to be lying to her. But why? What was hidden behind the Monk's Door that was so important?

*   *   *

Later that day Rosalind arrived, riding a sprightly little mare, in a tawny habit that made her eyes seem greener than ever. She sat, holding her mount in check, while Kitty stood at the door to greet her.

'Come on! I can see you're in your habit

already,' Rosalind called. 'Has Rupert found you a mount?'

'Yes, he's called Starlight, and I'm assured he's very gentle,' Kitty replied. A curious look crossed Rosalind's face, and she asked her new friend, 'Why, what is it?'

'Nothing. It's just that Starlight was Clorinda's horse,' Rosalind replied, and Kitty felt an icy finger touch her neck. Rupert had not mentioned that.

'Never mind. I'm not superstitious, and I'm sure Rupert would not have recommended Starlight for me if he did not think we would be suited to each other,' she said lightly.

Once mounted on Starlight, with the moorland tracks beneath her horse's feet, and the fresh wind in her face, Kitty felt a sense of exhilaration. She and Rosalind rode up to what Rosalind called the Crags, where huge stones, that looked as though they had been tossed there by some giant hand, towered over the surrounding countryside. There they stopped to rest their mounts, and seated themselves on some of the smaller stones.

'How beautiful! I can see that this is going to be one of my very favourite places. I shall come here when I want to be alone,' Kitty said, smiling. 'Not that I expect to want to be alone without Rupert very often.'

'You love him a great deal, don't you?' Rosalind asked casually, and Kitty flushed.

'Does it show that much?'

'My dear, it's written all over your face. One only has to look at the way you smile at him.' Rosalind picked a blade of grass, and chewed thoughtfully at the end of it. 'But I confess, I'm not entirely happy for you. If only I could be sure about—'

She stopped suddenly, so Kitty asked, 'Sure about what?'

Rosalind shook her head. 'No, I shouldn't have spoken. He has never given you any reason to doubt that he loves you just as much, has he?'

'No,' Kitty said, wondering exactly what the other girl meant.

'Well, that's all right, then,' Rosalind said, but her smile seemed forced.

Kitty sat up abruptly. 'Exactly what are you hinting at? Are you suggesting that Rupert doesn't love me? Then why would he want to marry me?'

Rosalind hesitated, staring out over the distant moors that merged with the horizon into a blue haze.

'I've known Rupert since he was young,' she said at last. 'He married Clorinda to please his father, you know.'

'Yes, he told me so,' Kitty said stiffly.

'But the reason why the old man wanted the match was because Clorinda was an orphan and an heiress, and he wanted to add her lands and property to the Fallows estate,' Rosalind went on. 'It was all put into the marriage

34

contract. So now Rupert should be a very wealthy man indeed.'

'Should be?' Kitty echoed incredulously. 'Do you means he's not?'

Rosalind played with her blade of grass. 'There's usually a year of mourning when a person is made a widow or a widower,' she pointed out. 'But it was only six months after the year was up that Rupert found himself another wife.'

'We fell in love,' Kitty retorted heatedly. 'He couldn't help it if he fell in love in such a short space of time!'

'But doesn't it strike you as convenient that he just happened to fall in love with Lady Katherine Mallory? Another heiress?' Rosalind asked softly, and Kitty felt the hot blood sting her cheeks.

'Are you suggesting that Rupert is marrying me for my money?' she inquired icily.

Rosalind put a hand on her arm. 'I'm just wondering,' she said, looking Kitty straight in the eyes. 'I want to be reassured, I suppose, that he really does care for you. I don't want you to be hurt, or unhappy, the same way—'

Again, she came to an abrupt halt, and Kitty finished challengingly, 'The same way that Clorinda was, were you going to say?'

'Well, he never pretended to love Clorinda, I'll give him that. They both knew it was a marriage of convenience,' Rosalind said, 'but he—well, could have done more to pretend he

35

cared a little. She was so young.'

Kitty stared. She could not imagine Rupert ever deliberately hurting the child-bride who smiled so sweetly from the picture above the fireplace in the Winter Parlour. Nor could she ever imagine that he would deliberately hurt her.

Kitty threw back her head. 'I don't believe for a moment that Rupert is marrying me for my money,' she declared. 'I'm sure you mean well, Rosalind, but Rupert loves me as I love him. He has no need of my fortune.'

'Possibly not. I hope you're right,' Rosalind answered, then looked up. 'But I must warn you, I've heard rumours that, when Rupert was in London, round about the time he met you, he had been really going to town in the worst sort of way. I'll spare you the details, but I'm sure you can imagine what a handsome, unattached man on the loose gets up to when he lets himself go. And the gossip runs that he's up to his ears in gambling debts!'

There was a moment's silence, then Kitty stood up and said in glacial tones, 'Rupert may regard you and your brother as some of his oldest friends, but if you can even listen to such outrageous lies, I regret I cannot ever consider you any friend of mine.'

She turned on her heel and strode towards her horse, but before she could mount, Rosalind was at her side, her arm plucking at Kitty's sleeve.

'Forgive me!' she begged, her green eyes pleading. 'I did not say I believed the gossip, just that I had heard it. And I am sure you know Rupert better than I do—after all, you have been betrothed to him for six months. I merely felt it was my duty to tell you what people are saying.'

Kitty turned and looked into the other girl's contrite face and her anger and shock subsided a little. She managed a smile.

'I'm sorry too,' she said. 'It was just that I could not imagine how such fanciful stories could have spread. I'm sure you were only concerned for me, but I can assure you, there is no need. I love Rupert, and he loves me, and we have no secrets from each other.'

'Then we are friends again?' Rosalind asked.

Kitty grasped her hands. 'Of course.'

'Oh, I could bite my tongue off,' the other girl said, pulling a face. 'Come, let's continue our ride. I want to show you one more place, then we'll go home.' As they mounted, she added, 'it's a remarkable feat of nature, a steep drop from an overhanging cliff. We call it the Chasm. You must be very careful to keep away from it when you are out riding on your own. I wanted to warn you about it.'

As they rode on, Kitty's thoughts were in a whirl. She did not believe what Rosalind had said to her, yet how in the world had such terrible tales come to be spread about

Rupert? For a moment, just a moment, she wondered whether she really knew Rupert, or whether it was true that he was a philanderer without scruples, that he was a gambler, that he was marrying her for her money. Then, almost instantly, she dismissed the doubts as unworthy.

All the same, she decided, in a little corner of her mind, she would do her best to discover whether any of the things Rosalind had said could possibly be true, without, of course, giving Rupert any indication of the tales she had heard.

She viewed the staggering, breathtaking drop from the Chasm with no particular emotion, her mind still filled with troubled queries concerning Rupert, and was thankful that Rosalind had shown the place to her so that she could beware of it. If she had come out alone, she might have stumbled across it by accident before anyone warned her, and met with a dreadful accident, possibly even death.

The thought sent a shiver down her spine, and it was with genuine relief that she followed as the other girl led the way back to Fallows. There was something reassuring in the sight of the tall chimneys with which she was becoming familiar.

She invited Rosalind in for luncheon, but the other declined, saying she was not dressed to visit anyone indoors.

'I must be getting home myself,' Rosalind

told her, and with a return of her bubbling high spirits, she waved her crop as she turned her horse. 'I'll come by one day soon for tea. And, of course, you must pay a visit to us. Good-bye, dear Kitty.'

CHAPTER FOUR

When she saw Rupert waiting for her, her heart gave its usual leap of gladness, but at the same time, she wondered whether, after this morning, she would ever be able to look at him in the same complete light of adoration as previously, or whether a tiny, niggling sense of doubt would persist in the back of her mind. For the shock of Rosalind's words was still reverberating in her brain.

'Darling! Did you have a good ride?' he asked as he kissed her, before leading her into the cool of the dining-room, where the windows were open to let in the breeze, and the drapes moved gently. Even in her light, muslin gown, Kitty could feel the sultry air, and the sunshine outside seemed to flood the garden with brilliance.

'Rosalind took me to the Crags, and to show me a place called the Chasm, which she warned me to beware of,' Kitty answered, as they seated themselves, and Rupert's face grew anxious.

'I meant to take you to the Chasm myself, and to give you instructions—no, forbid you ever to ride near the place alone,' he declared, and Kitty could not help wondering briefly whether his concern was genuine, or feigned. However, he seemed so preoccupied with her welfare, so loving, so tender and considerate, that she could not doubt him.

The maid came in with the first course and, as she picked up her spoon, Kitty broached the subject uppermost in her mind.

'You spend so much of your time caring for me, Rupert. What did you do before you met me? When you were in London, for instance?'

'I wandered like a lost soul searching for happiness,' he answered, his eyes darkening. 'I had lost my father—, and my mother long since. And then Clorinda. I wondered whether I would ever know companionship again, or whether I would be alone for the rest of my life.'

'You didn't mingle much with society while you were in London, then?' Kitty persisted.

He shrugged. 'Oh, I attended the usual functions, went to the opera, and so on,' he replied. 'And I attended such balls and parties as I was invited to—I'm afraid I was considered rather eligible, and many anxious Mamas were eager to have their daughters become the second Lady Hamill.'

Kitty laughed, trying to make a joke of it. 'You didn't have any special lady friends before me, did you? Or drown your sorrows in drink, or—or gambling?' she inquired.

'What a dreadful character you are painting of me!' he responded, grinning at her. 'But I can assure you that your fears are unfounded, love. None of the young women who crowded around me ever attracted me in the slightest—before you. And as for drinking and gambling—what do you want me to say? Would it make you view me in a better light— give me a little more attraction in your eyes— if I were to confess to you that I had drunk and gambled away my nights?'

'You didn't, did you?' Kitty asked, genuinely alarmed, and he laughed out loud at the expression on her face.

'Of course I didn't, but I couldn't help teasing you, darling. I thought you might have had a secret desire to find that you had reformed a rakehell. But I'm afraid I lived very quietly and soberly.'

'I'm glad,' Kitty said, and she spoke from the bottom of her heart. No matter how the vicious tales of Rupert's gambling and philandering had arisen, she had his own word—which she believed—that he was as she had always known him, decent, upright and true as the day.

It was as if a burden had lifted from her shoulders, and she passed the rest of the afternoon walking with him in the sunshine to the village, and inspecting the charming

41

old church where she would be married, in utter contentment. Only one small incident happened to cast a cloud across her sky.

They were in the churchyard, when Rupert said quietly, 'Clorinda is buried here, along with my parents and other ancestors, in the family vault. Do you want to see it?'

'I should like to see where Clorinda is buried,' Kitty answered, with only a trace of reluctance. She did not like the sound of the words 'family vault.' It reminded her that one day, when she died, she too would be brought here and laid amongst the other Hamill dead, and she shivered, even though the sun was hot. But she felt it to be her duty in some way to visit Clorinda's resting-place, and she wished she had thought to bring some flowers.

When they turned the corner to the back of the church, however, and she saw the forbidding marble vault, like a small house, she realised there was no need for her to bring flowers. A wreath of fresh blooms, sweetly scented, had been hung from the handle of the great door that led into the vault. Rupert frowned.

'That's odd,' he said, as they stepped carefully through among the gravestones, and he bent to inspect the wreath. A card was attached to it.

'What does it say?' Kitty asked, intrigued. If Rupert had not laid a wreath in memory of his first bride, then who had? She knew that

42

Clorinda had had no relatives. 'Who is it for?'

Rupert read out slowly, 'And the dead shall arise.'

A chill prickled Kitty's bare arms. 'Is there no name?' she asked.

He shook his head. 'That's all that's written here. But what a strange thing to write. And who is the wreath meant for? Hardly for my parents. It must be in memory of Clorinda.'

'That was what I thought,' Kitty said. 'But if you did not put it here, Rupert, nor authorise anyone else to do so, then who did?'

'I have no idea. No one has ever placed flowers here before,' Rupert said, and she could see that he was puzzled. 'Besides, it's two years since Clorinda passed away. Why lay flowers here for her now, after all this time?'

'I wonder why they chose those particular words to write on the card,' Kitty murmured, uneasily. 'About the dead arising, I mean. It's, well, a little frightening.'

His arm went round her shoulders. 'Don't let it upset you, love. If someone loved Clorinda, and wants to pay their respects, I have no objection. And I firmly believe that the dead are at peace.'

'You think Clorinda rests quietly?' Kitty said, still uneasy, and he held her close.

'I'm certain of it. Come, let's go home. I'm sorry I brought you here to see the vault. You need not come again in the future.'

Kitty's uneasiness over the wreath had been completely dispelled by the time they arrived back at the house, where Mrs Potter had tea ready, and she ate with a hearty appetite, the fresh air having made her hungry. Afterwards, she and Rupert spent a quiet evening, content in each other's company, and by ten o'clock, Kitty was yawning.

'What with riding this morning, and walking this afternoon, I am ridiculously tired,' she apologised. 'It must be the fresh air.'

Rupert smiled and said, 'Then you must retire, love.'

Kitty agreed. She smothered another yawn. 'I can hardly keep my eyes open. Goodnight, my love. You need not come with me to my door, I can find my way now. I'll ring for Lucy, and go to bed.'

She and Rupert exchanged tender kisses before she left the drawing-room, and made her way up the stairs and along the corridors in the still faint light of the dying day. Her bed looked particularly comfortable, and when Lucy came in answer to her bell, she prepared for bed as quickly as possible. After the maid had gone, she relaxed into the soft down of her mattress. In a very short time, she had fallen into a peaceful sleep.

She awoke to find moonlight streaming through the window. She had bidden Lucy to leave the curtains open, so that she would catch the fragrant night air with its coolness. Kitty found that her heart was thudding uneasily. As she raised herself upon one elbow, she wondered what had frightened her, what had woken her. Every sense alert, she listened.

The curtains whispered softly in the slight breeze, then Kitty's tense nerves jumped as she heard another sound, seemingly outside her door. It sounded like a moan, low and long-drawn-out and, within a few seconds, it was followed by another.

She was thankful for the bright silver light as she fumblingly lit a candle, and called out, 'Who's there?'

She was very conscious that there was no lock upon her door, and that anyone could come in. As she waited, the moan came again, but the door handle remained untouched.

Kitty's uneasiness and fright were giving way to curiosity. Who, among the servants, was likely to wander her corridor, moaning as though her heart was breaking? She got out of bed and slid into her robe, then went to the door and listened. Everything was very still now. Then, a long way off, she heard the moan again, and she flung open the door to find the corridor empty. But—she spun round—there was unmistakably the sound of footsteps on wood, the shuffle of slippers, and she ran, her candle throwing out a comforting glow, in the direction of the Monk's Door.

As she turned the corner, she could see that it stood wide open, and she knew that someone had just gone up the Monk's Stairs. They had seemed very solid beneath her feet when she had ventured up them the first time, and she did not believe they were unsafe. Lifting the skirt of her nightgown and robe, she hurried up the stairs, emerging, panting, on the landing.

The three doors were still shut, but she was certain she had heard one of them close as she had run barefooted up the wooden steps. Which one was it? She tried each door in turn, but none would give. Then she stood and listened again. The quiet seemed absolute at first, but then she heard a quick, indrawn breath from behind one of the doors, and called softly, 'Who's there? Who is it? Come out, please, I'd like to help you. Are you in trouble?'

Again she waited. Though there was no reply to her words, she was certain that just behind one of the doors, another person was standing, ear strained for the slightest sound, as she herself was.

She tried again. 'Please let me help. Open the door, won't you?'

Silence, then there was a muffled cry, as though someone had tried to call out, and been abruptly stopped by a hand pushed across her mouth. At least, Kitty guessed it to be a woman; the voice had sounded high and thin. And the words she had heard had been "Let me—Let me, what?"

Convinced by now that someone was in trouble, that perhaps one of the younger maids was in some disgrace or difficulty, and she had been in the process of being scolded by Mrs Potter, or one of her superior, who did not want the master's fiancée to hear what was going on, Kitty went back down the stairs, determined to wake Rupert and find out what was happening.

As she went through the Monk's Door, however, she came to a sudden stop. Two things happened simultaneously. Her candle blew out, leaving her in blackness, and at the same time, a loud laugh, which made her hair rise at the sheer inhumanity of it, came from somewhere very close at hand. Then she sensed, rather than felt, the blow on her head, before she fell forward into the dazzle of red stars that preceded unconsciousness.

*   *   *

Lucy came scurrying along the corridor in response to the frenzied jangling of Kitty's bell, a hastily-lit candle in her shaking hand. Whatever could have befallen her mistress? She burst into the room, then stopped in horror as she saw Kitty lying on the floor, in her nightgown, tears streaming down her face tugging desperately at the long bell cord.

'My lady, my lady, whatever happened?' Lucy gasped, assisting Kitty to the bed.

'Get Sir Rupert—hurry, Lucy—call him—rouse the house—Mrs Potter—' But as Lucy made for the door, her voice rose to a scream. 'No, don't go! Don't leave me alone!'

'How else can I get the master, my lady?' Lucy demanded in distress, wringing her hands.

Kitty made a great effort. 'Go then. But hurry, please hurry!'

Lights sprung to bloom as the household was aroused, and Rupert strode quickly to Kitty's room in the wake of the running Lucy. Mrs Potter, in a sedate, dark robe, followed at his heels. They found that Kitty had now managed to control her sobs, but there were tear-marks on her face, and Rupert, careless of proprieties, swept her into his arms as he sat beside her on the bed.

'Dearest! My love, what has upset you so?'

'I was attacked. Somebody attacked me. My candle went out, and then I heard a laugh—dear God, such a laugh, as though the devils of Hell were let loose—and he—she—hit me on the head,' Kitty tried to speak coherently, but it was only after Rupert had held her against his breast for some time, and Mrs Potter had slipped quietly away to return with a soothing herbal cordial, that she managed to tell the whole of her story.

Rupert turned to Mrs Potter as soon as she

mentioned the Monk's Door.

'That confounded door! Take the lamp and investigate, Mrs Potter—no, wait a moment. If we have an intruder at large, you may not be safe. Robbs must go with you.'

'I'm here, sir,' the butler's voice came from the corridor. He was hovering discreetly, carrying a large poker.

'Go and see what's happening in those rooms up the Monk's Stairs,' Rupert commanded, and continued to try to comfort Kitty, who was still clinging to him.

In a few moments, the two were back

'Well?' Rupert barked.

Mrs Potter shook her head bewilderedly. 'The Monk's Door is shut and locked, as it was when we tried it the other day, sir,' she reported, and Robbs gave confirmation of her report. Rupert turned to Kitty, who was starting from his arms, dismay written upon her face.

'It can't be—I tell you there was someone there, up in one of the rooms, I know there was,' she faltered, and Rupert stroked her hair, frowning. Kitty turned to him in growing agitation. 'I have a lump on my head where I was hit—here, feel it,' she pleaded, guiding his fingers to the bruise that made her wince.

'You certainly knocked your head on something,' he admitted, examining her scalp beneath the flowing locks very carefully. 'There's no blood, though, thank God.'

49

'But doesn't that prove what I say? That my story is true?' Kitty demanded, and Rupert hesitated. Then he turned to Lucy, who was standing by, the picture of dismay.

'Where was your mistress when you found her? Tell me exactly, Lucy,' he commanded gently.

'She was lying on the floor by the bell, sir, tugging at the bell cord,' she replied without hesitation.

'But of course, when I came to at the end of the corridor, I had to get back in order to summon help,' Kitty cried. 'I crawled back on my hands and knees in the dark, and then just pulled on the bell until Lucy came.'

'Isn't it possible that you might have simply had a very bad dream, love, and perhaps fallen from your bed, hitting your head, so that when you regained consciousness, you thought you had been attacked, and crawled across the floor, in your fright, to ring the bell?' Rupert suggested, stroking Kitty's cheek tenderly. 'The Monk's Door is shut, there is no sign of any intruder—though we will get the men to check the whole house before we retire to bed again, Robbs—and Lucy found you here in your room. I hardly think you could have opened a locked door, and met some strange person who wanted to hide from you up the Monk's Stairs. And I can imagine no-one who would have attacked you so viciously, my darling. You are among friends, you are safe,

50

this is your home, or soon will be.'

'Where is my candlestick then?' Kitty demanded, with a flash of triumph. 'It must have fallen from my hand as I fell. I did go along the corridor, just as I have said.'

Wordlessly, Rupert pointed to her candlestick, standing on the tallboy.

'I picked it up myself when I came in, sir,' Mrs Potter said quietly. 'It had rolled beneath the bed, and was only half visible.'

'You see, darling?' Rupert insisted. 'Even your candlestick never left your room.'

Kitty hid her face in her hands. What was the use? They would never believe her. She knew that what had happened that night was not a product of her imagination, but she was calmer now, and she decided to say nothing further, but to investigate on her own in the morning.

'Yes, you must be right,' she said humbly. 'I am so sorry to have disturbed everyone.'

'Don't worry about that, darling. If there is an intruder in the house we'll find him,' Rupert said, setting his lips grimly. 'Can you go and organise the men for a search, Robbs?'

'Yes, my lord,' Robbs declared, and disappeared.

Rupert tucked Kitty up among the bedclothes, and she said firmly, 'I want a lock put on my door tomorrow, and the lamp left burning for the rest of the night. I shan't sleep a wink, I know I shan't.'

'You will, my lady. The herbs I gave you will help you to sleep,' Mrs Potter assured her, while Rupert threw back the curtains, which someone had drawn while Kitty was telling her story.

'Good. Thank you, Mrs Potter,' Rupert said, sitting beside Kitty once more, and taking her hand. 'I suppose you have not yet come across the key to the Monk's Door?' he added, frowning. 'This is the second time that Lady Katherine has imagined she saw it open—or was able to open it. It is possible that some servant may be playing tricks if the key is in circulation.'

Mrs Potter held herself with dignity. 'After the last time, sir, I particularly asked them about it and went through all the keys I know of in the hour. The lock upon the Monk's Door is large and would require an especially large key,' she told him. 'But I can find no one who has any knowledge of the door ever being opened, and no key that fits the lock.'

'There you are then, my darling,' Rupert said to Kitty. 'You see, it must be all in your imagination. But why this particular door should so fascinate you, I cannot think.'

Kitty said nothing. She was not altogether certain that Mrs Potter was telling the truth—and yet, why should the housekeeper be lying?

'Did you ever have fancies like this before you came to Fallows?' Rupert asked gently. 'I would not have suspected that you were of a

52

nervous disposition. You have always seemed eminently sensible to me before.'

'I don't have fancies,' Kitty protested indignantly. 'Neither am I of a nervous disposition.'

But Rupert was looking at her with a strange expression, and she had a surge of anger. Could he possibly imagine her mind was unhinged?

'For Heaven's sake, just because I have a few bad dreams, it doesn't mean I'm going mad,' she snapped, with a flash of spirit. And Rupert gave a laugh that was only a little strained.

'My darling, I assure you, I was not even hinting at such a thing.' He kissed her contritely. 'It is perfectly understandable that in a strange house, and such an old house, you should have a few disturbed nights. And as for my hinting that you were of a nervous disposition, I can see now that this is my Kitty as I know her, and I beg your forgiveness.'

'Of course,' Kitty said softly, aware that they had almost quarrelled, for the first time in their relationship, and he rose.

'I am tiring you, and you need rest. Sleep now, darling, and this time, have happy dreams.'

'I'll dream of you,' Kitty said, blowing him a kiss, as she lay back against the pillows. Rupert and Mrs Potter withdrew, and in the pearly light of dawn, Kitty sank back to sleep.

CHAPTER FIVE

Nothing disturbed Kitty's slumbers for the next few hours, but when Lucy came with a late cup of tea for her, having left her to rest for longer than usual, she dressed thoughtfully and, when she had dismissed Lucy, decided to go and have a look at the Monk's Door—for she was still certain she had not dreamed the happenings of the night.

The door was closed and locked this time, but her painstaking search of the square of thin carpet outside it yielded what, to her, was proof that the attack on her had been real. For she found, as she felt the carpet with her hand, a small patch of encrusted candle grease, which must have run from her candlestick when it fell from her hand. It was fresh and new, undisturbed.

Slowly, Kitty stood up. What could possibly be happening in this house? It was obvious that someone did possess the key to the Monk's Door, and to the doors at the top of the stairs. Was it Rupert? He had hinted that she might be slightly mad. Was he trying to frighten her into madness, yet pretending he had no knowledge of what was going on? Or was it Mrs Potter, who was keeping some secret behind the locked door to herself? Or was it some faceless adversary, who intended harm to her?

When the post-bag was delivered that day, there was a letter to Kitty from her mama, bubbling with plans about the wedding, which made her smile. Dear, empty-headed Mama!

An exclamation from Rupert made her look up. He was frowning over a letter.

'What is it?'

'It appears that I have to go to York on business, darling,' he told her. 'I must leave as soon as possible and may be gone for two or three days. And just as you have arrived! It's most inconvenient, but I must go, as it concerns estate business.'

'But of course you must go, if it is necessary,' Kitty assured him, trying to speak cheerfully. 'But I shall miss you, darling.'

He put down the letter and placed his hands on her shoulders, his blue eyes on her face.

'I'll hurry back, Kitty. I can't bear to be parted from you even for a moment now.'

Careless of any servants who might come in, he then gave her a long and lingering kiss on the lips.

'Always remember, I love you,' he said softly, and she felt her heart turn over, as she returned his declaration of affection. Then he had to leave the room to make arrangements for travelling to York, and Kitty did not see him again, until he was packed and ready in his travelling clothes.

He gave her only a quick kiss, on the cheek,

since there were servants watching, and she stood on the steps by the front door as the carriage rumbled off down the drive, Rupert waving his handkerchief from the window to her until the turn in the trees took him out of her sight.

She wandered back into the house, feeling more alone than she had expected, and sat down a short time later to a solitary luncheon. What should she do with herself? She could pay a visit to the Meade's but, though she would have liked to see Rosalind, the thought of Sebastian and his unfortunate attachment to her made her reluctant to go there, especially without Rupert's company.

Restlessly, she decided to pluck some flowers from the garden, and arrange them. It was when she was busy later in the little flower room that Robbs announced a visitor.

'A visitor?' Kitty said, turning in surprise.

'Doctor Parsons has called, my lady,' Robbs intoned.

Immediately, Kitty felt her spirits rise. She had taken a liking to the young doctor.

'Show him into the drawing-room, please, Robbs, and tell him I shall be with him directly,' she ordered, and as the butler bowed himself out, she hurried up to her room to freshen herself and tidy her hair. Then she went down.

Edward Parsons, who was seated on the edge of a delicate chair, rose immediately she

56

entered the room.

'Doctor Parsons, how good of you to call.' Kitty smiled, extending her hand, and he brushed her fingers with his lips ceremoniously.

'I hope I am not intruding in any way?'

'Indeed not, quite the contrary. May I offer you some tea?' Kitty said, as they both seated themselves comfortably, and he returned her smile.

'That would be extremely pleasant.'

Kitty rang the bell and ordered tea and sandwiches for two, then turned her attention to the doctor.

'It would be very rude of me not to make Rupert's friends welcome,' she declared, and explained how Rupert had been called away to York, adding, 'I am quite at a loss without him. Your calling could not have been at a more fortunate moment.'

'It's a pleasant change to be able to make a social visit instead of being here in my professional capacity,' the doctor told her, and Kitty felt a stirring of interest.

'Yes, I understand that you attended the first Lady Hamill—Clorinda—during her last illness. It must have been a very distressing time for you, especially her tragic end,' she said, deliberately leading him into telling her about Clorinda's death. 'I imagine that to lose her and her child would have been extremely painful, for you were a friend as well as a

57

medical adviser to her, were you not?'

He looked both grave and surprised.

'It was a sad time for all her friends, Lady Katherine. But, of course, you would not have been told that it was not I who was with her during that fatal night.'

Kitty stared. 'But you were her doctor? Rupert told me you were constantly in the house during her illness.'

'That is true. For several months before her confinement, she kept to her bed, on my advice, and I visited her regularly,' he explained. 'But as her time grew near, I felt I was not able to give her the attention she required, and recommended that another doctor be called in to stay in the house in case any emergency should arise when her child was born.

'What actually happened on the night that Clorinda—Lady Hamill—passed away, I am not exactly certain, for, as I had recommended, a doctor from London was called in, and lived here in the house. But Clorinda's child was born prematurely, and I was, as I had predicted, attending to another case when labour commenced, so the birth and its attendant tragedy were dealt with entirely by Doctor Smith and, I believe, Mrs Potter. By the time I arrived on the scene, Clorinda was already in her coffin in the drawing-room, and the tiny body of the dead child with her.'

'How terribly tragic!' Kitty murmured,

sincerely. 'You must have felt sad as you looked at her poor dead face. I hope she did not suffer too much.'

She knew she was dwelling, in what might have seemed a morbid fashion, on the subject of Clorinda's death, but she felt that she wanted to know everything she could discover about her predecessor, and Edward Parsons did not appear to find her preoccupation unusual. He was thinking back over two years, shaking his head sombrely.

'I did not see her face, Lady Katherine. The coffin had already been sealed.'

Kitty felt a prickle of alarm creep up her spine. 'But surely that was very strange? You must have come quite soon after she died.'

'The day after,' he agreed. 'But Doctor Smith had already departed back to London, and Clorinda had already been prepared for her last journey to the family vault, and the coffin sealed, as I have said.'

'How odd,' Kitty said slowly. 'Why was there the need for such unusual haste? So that even her friends were not able to pay their last respects? Have you any idea?'

'None at all. Unless it was because of Rupert's grief,' the doctor told her, and Kitty, torn between the subject of Rupert's grief and the mysterious sealing of Clorinda's coffin, clasped her hands and decided to confide in Edward Parsons, whom she felt instinctively as a friend.

'Doctor Parsons,' she began. 'I would like to be quite frank with you. I have heard rumours that—that Clorinda was not happy as Rupert's wife. You were her physician. You would surely have known if this was the case. I confess, I am troubled by these rumours, when I am about to become Rupert's wife myself. Can you give me any information, however brief, which will help to ease my mind?'

The tea and sandwiches were brought in at that moment, and while the maid set out the tea-tray on a small table between them, the young doctor seemed to be deep in thought.

At length, after the maid had bobbed a curtsey and left the room, he looked up at Kitty, who was pouring the tea, and said, 'I don't know exactly what rumours you have heard, Lady Katherine, but if it will help, I can tell you that Clorinda was a very confused child—for she was little more. She told me that strange things happened to her—odd things. She mislaid various possessions, for instance, and later discovered them in their rightful places. And she said, she heard strange voices, and saw, well, I suppose the right term would be ghosts, or spirits.'

Kitty could hardly believe her ears. Had Clorinda, too, been persecuted, as she was, by some strange assailant?

'And what did you make of her revelations, Doctor Parsons?' she asked carefully. 'Did she say they happened in any particular part of the house, or just generally?' For in her mind, of course, was a vivid picture of the Monk's Door, and the staircase behind it.

Edward Parsons took the tea she handed him, and sighed. 'No, she did not associate them with anywhere in particular,' he answered. 'They seemed to happen in different places—sometimes when she was not even indoors. And as to what conclusions I came to, well, I confess, I did not believe she was lying to me, but I was forced to conclude that she had an especially nervous disposition, and that many of the things she said she saw and heard were the product of an over-stimulated imagination.

'As to the rest—' he shrugged, 'she was extremely sensitive, and I could only presume that she allowed small details to assume large proportions in her mind, and translated them into vivid happenings she believed to be important, when, in fact, they were trivial.'

Kitty was in a whirl of suppressed emotion. This was the last thing she had expected to hear, and now, of course, she could understand Rupert's anxiety when he had inquired whether she had fancies or was unduly sensitive. He was afraid that she would begin to behave as Clorinda had, in a way that to any ordinary person, must have seemed almost mad. Yet she was convinced that Clorinda had not been mad, but had been subjected to the same strange ordeals she had experienced herself.

It appeared that there was someone who resented Rupert being married, and was determined to cause distress, first his wife and then, after Clorinda's death, to his fiancée. But who in the world could it be—and why?

Kitty looked thoughtful. 'Just one more thing,' she said. 'And then I will stop bothering you about the details of Clorinda's illness. Did she—did she ever say that she thought someone was persecuting her? Causing these things to happen, I mean? Did she have any idea who it was?'

He pondered, hesitated, then said slowly, 'If it were not for the fact that you are soon to marry Rupert and become a member of his family, I would not tell you this. But she seemed to be under the impression that it was his mother who was responsible—a ridiculous idea, as you will agree, since his mother had died when he was very young.'

Kitty tried to suppress the horror and shock his words brought to her. She understood, only too well, that to him the idea must have seemed fanciful, but to Kitty it was clear that the pattern was repeating itself over again; for was it not a dead woman, Clorinda herself, who seemed to be visiting her?

'There is no family legend about this, is there?' she asked quickly. 'About the last mistress of the house haunting the next, as it were?'

He shook his head, pursing his lips. 'Certainly not. And, personally, I do not believe in ghosts, Lady Katherine. No, the simple fact was that—I am sorry to say it—but Clorinda's mind was disturbed.'

What about mine? Kitty thought to herself wryly. But she thanked the young doctor for his confidences and assured him she would be utterly discreet about what he had told her, and they finished off speaking of trivialities, and the life of the village in general, before he took his leave.

CHAPTER SIX

Though Kitty was apprehensive with Rupert away from home, nothing untoward occurred that night, and the next day, she decided she simply must confide in someone. The person who sprang to her mind was Rosalind, and, braving the possibility of meeting Sebastian, she rode over to the Meades' after luncheon, and found Rosalind on her own, playing the pianoforte in the rather shabby, but comfortable drawing-room.

To her relief, Rosalind expressed great delight to see her, and told her that her mama and Sebastian had gone to visit a relative in the nearest town.

'And Papa is at the mill, of course,'

Rosalind added, and her bubbling smile swept Kitty up. 'But come in, dearest Kitty, the groom will see to your horse. I want an excuse for not practising my usual hour at the piano, and you will do admirably. How lovely to see you. You'll have some tea, of course?'

'A little later, if you don't mind, as it is not long since I had luncheon,' Kitty said, warmed by the other girl's welcome, as she seated herself in a chair by the window that looked out over a charming old-world garden. It was just a fraction untidy, as was the house, and Kitty found it a relief not to be on her best behaviour, as she felt she should be at Fallows, much though she loved Rupert's family home.

Rosalind sat opposite her, smiling with pleasure. 'How delightful! Now we can have a real tête-à-tête,' she enthused. 'You can tell me all about your wedding plans, Kitty dear.'

'Well, actually, I have something else I would like to talk to you about,' Kitty said, rather hesitantly. She looked round. 'There is no chance of our being overheard?'

'Oh, no. Cook and Sarah are in the kitchen, and there is no one else in the house,' Rosalind said, and her green eyes sparkled. 'We don't live in such tremendous style as you do at Fallows, you know, with an army of slaves to wait on our every whim.'

Kitty tried to smile at the joke, but her eyes were troubled, and Rosalind immediately sensed her mood.

'Has something happened? Is anything wrong?' she asked in concern.

Kitty hesitated, then said slowly, 'I'm not sure.'

She told the other girl of Edward Parsons' visit, and what he had said about Clorinda hearing and seeing things, and Rosalind listened in growing amazement.

'I knew there was something wrong, but I did not know it was so distressing,' she said, when Kitty had finished. 'Poor Clorinda. No wonder she often appeared distracted and unhappy. But why should this bother you, Kitty? You did not even know her.'

Kitty leaned forward, her fingers clenched together. 'Because the same thing is happening to me,' she said, in a low voice. 'I have the same feeling that Clorinda had, but it is not Rupert's mother, it is Clorinda herself who seems to haunt me. I smell her scent, I found her gloves laid out in place of my own. And— and I have seen things too which everyone assures me must be only dreams. On one occasion, I was attacked, and hit over the head, but nobody at Fallows believes I ever left my room. They think I fell out of bed and knocked myself, in the middle of a bad dream.'

Rosalind stared. 'You think Clorinda is trying to harm you?' she asked.

Kitty shook her head doubtfully. 'No, apart from that one blow over the head, I don't think I am in any danger. But someone—or

65

something—is playing tricks on me, and I'm convinced that it was the same with Clorinda. I don't believe her mind was disturbed. I believe that similar tricks were played upon her too, to make her—and everyone round her—think she was nervous and imaginative. But who, and why, I have no idea.'

'It's such a fantastic story,' Rosalind said, after a moment.

Kitty looked up quickly. 'Then you don't believe me either?'

'Yes, of course I do, you aren't the sort of person to start seeing things when they're not there. But who can be responsible for trying to make you seem—well, mad? And what would be the point of it?' Rosalind asked.

Kitty shrugged. 'I hoped you might be able to come up with some idea that would help. I had to confide in someone, and I fear that everyone at Fallows must be suspect. I'm inclined to think, for instance, that Mrs Potter is involved in some way, for I have seen her behaving in a manner that makes me feel she knows more than she says she does.'

'But surely she wouldn't do such things on her own initiative?' Rosalind pointed out. 'She is only a servant, after all, and she would be dismissed if she was found out. Have you told Rupert your suspicions?'

Kitty shook her head. 'No, how can I? I told him I had been through the Monk's Door, and heard someone in one of the rooms at the top of the stairs, but the door is locked and they say there is no key.'

'The Monk's Door has always been locked, as far as I know,' Rosalind agreed.

'That is what they keep telling me,' Kitty said in exasperation. 'But twice now, I swear I have found it open and gone up the stairs. I did not imagine it, I know I went up the Monk's Stairs and that there was someone in one of the rooms. Probably more than one person, for it sounded as though someone tried to cry out to me, and was prevented.'

Rosalind thought deeply for several moments, then she ventured slowly, 'What if—this is just an idea, you understand—what if Clorinda really was unbalanced? And her nervous fancies gave someone the inspiration to try to frighten you, or at least, make it seem as though you were unbalanced too?'

'But who?' Kitty asked desperately. Rosalind did not speak for a few moments, then she said very seriously, 'I hate to say this, but Rupert is the master of the house. Has it occurred to you that it might be Rupert himself who is responsible for arranging your strange happenings, with the assistance, perhaps, of Mrs Potter?'

'Rupert?' Kitty echoed, aghast at the very idea.

Rosalind was tapping her fingers against the top of a small table beside her chair, as she wrestled with her thoughts.

'It might even have been Rupert who played the same tricks on poor Clorinda,' she said at last. 'That's if her mind really was not unbalanced. I told you he married her for her fortune. Perhaps he wanted to get rid of her, so he tried to drive her insane, once he had her money.'

'But she died in childbirth,' Kitty protested, with a sinking feeling in her heart. It all sounded so plausible.

There was a pause, then Rosalind pointed out, 'Yes, but who was with her when her child was born? Mrs Potter and the doctor from London. The doctor could have been an accomplice of Rupert's. It is so easy for a woman to die in childbirth.'

'But that would be—' Kitty began, then stopped and hid her face in her hands, too horrified even to contemplate that her beloved Rupert might be a cold-blooded murderer. It could not be! There must be some other explanation.

Then a thought struck her, and she said quickly, 'but it can't be Rupert who is trying to make it seem that I'm unbalanced. If we were already married, and he had my fortune, I could understand the motive, but we will not be man and wife for several weeks, so why should he play foolish pranks on me now, before I am safely wed to him?'

'Perhaps to establish a sort of pattern?' Rosalind said, though her tone was doubtful.

'To make it seem as though you were just slightly odd before the marriage, so that afterwards, when he is in possession of your money, he will be able to increase the tricks, and make them more dangerous, and then, at last, rid himself of you in some way?'

'I can't believe he would ever harm me,' Kitty burst out, incredulously, but at the same time, a memory flashed into her mind of when she had told Rupert about Sebastian's threat to take her away from her betrothed, and he had said, 'I think I would kill him. Or perhaps, kill you.'

'I've just thought of something else,' Rosalind said, and her voice made Kitty grow cold. 'After Clorinda died, no one was allowed to view the body. The coffin was sealed up immediately, and even we, who had been her friends, could not pay our last respects to her. And the doctor from London left the house before daylight, that frightful morning. We wondered at the time why Rupert authorised the coffin to be sealed so quickly, but perhaps it was to hide the evidence of whatever had happened to her during the night.'

Kitty found these words, which echoed almost exactly what Edward Parsons had told her, almost too much to bear.

'It can't be true! It can't!' she cried. 'I won't believe Rupert is a murderer!

'Well, there's only one other explanation, isn't there?' Rosalind said.

'What?' Kitty asked.

'Why, that there was no body in the coffin at all,' were the staggering words Rosalind pronounced. 'That Clorinda did not die. That it is she, herself, who is playing these tricks on you!'

*　　　　*　　　　*

In the cool of the summer evening, Kitty wandered slowly in the walled garden at Fallows, pondering deeply on the events of the day. The revelations of the young doctor, and her conversation with Rosalind had shaken her so that she felt she required peace and seclusion until she had managed to sort out her tumbled thoughts.

One thing she could not accept was that Clorinda still lived. There was the strange gipsy's warning to beware, and the perfume, the gloves, the mysterious personage in the locked room. All these seemed to give credence to Rosalind's words, but Kitty could not bring herself to believe that Rupert, her dearly loved betrothed, was preparing himself to commit bigamy and marry a second wife while his first still lived. He had had such pain in his face when he spoke of her death that she was convinced that Clorinda must be dead. She had to be.

But how she had come to die, and whether it had indeed been Rupert who had been responsible and who was now fabricating the tricks that were being played upon her, was a different matter. She could not dismiss this aspect so lightly. Could one person really know another? Did she really know Rupert? Was he the ardent lover he seemed to be, or was it all a facade, intended to deceive her? Should she leave Fallows now, cancel the wedding, and forget Rupert?

But, as she stood looking at the lovely old house, with the evening scents from the garden drifting to her in delicate clouds, and thought of the face she loved so much, and his arms around her, she knew she could not. Her heart and soul had been given to Rupert and his home.

*   *   *

She slept fitfully, but once again, nothing occurred during the night, and an inner doubt crossed her mind that perhaps it was because Rupert was away, and unable to play any pranks upon her, but she dismissed the thought firmly as she dressed the next morning. Then, a few hours later, she was engaged in writing a letter to her mother when she heard a bustle in the hall, footsteps upon the black and white tiles, all the sounds of arrival, and her spirits lifted involuntarily as she hurried out of the library. Rupert had come home!

He was looking round for her, and when he saw her, his face lit up, and he swept her off her feet into his arms.

'Darling Kitty! How I have missed you!'

'I've missed you too,' she admitted, as his presence seemed to penetrate through the quiet of the house, bringing it to life. 'Did you have a good journey? And were your business affairs conducted satisfactorily?'

He was stroking her hair, careless of the servants who were bringing in his bags, then he kissed her forehead.

'Yes, my love, all is well. But you—how have you been? I hurried home as quickly as I could.'

'The time has passed pleasantly enough,' Kitty said, and could not help adding, 'except that you were not here.' As they walked through into the drawing-room, she told him, 'The doctor called, and I rode over to see Rosalind Meade yesterday.'

'So you're making friends. I'm glad about that.' He smiled, then turned as Mrs Potter entered the room and stood in her usual dignified posture, with her hands folded. 'Yes, Mrs Potter? What is it?'

'Will you be requiring refreshments, sir?' the housekeeper asked calmly. 'Or shall I wait and have tea served at the usual time? Lady Katherine has already had luncheon.'

'I'm ravenous, Mrs Potter. I didn't stop for luncheon, I was in such a hurry to return

72

home,' Rupert said.

'A meal will be ready in the dining-room in about twenty minutes, sir.'

'Ah, just the thing. But serve it in the Winter Parlour, if you don't mind, Mrs Potter,' Rupert told her. 'I don't feel like sitting formally in the dining-room. I have a lot to say to my fiancée, and the Winter Parlour will be more cosy.'

'Very good, sir,' Mrs Potter intoned, and made a discreet exit. Rupert took Kitty into his arms and kissed her face with a barely restrained passion.

'I could eat you too, you darling creature.' He laughed. 'But I kept telling myself that each day brought our wedding morning closer.' Then his face grew serious. 'You haven't been troubled by anything while I was away? No more bad dreams?'

'No, nothing,' Kitty admitted, wondering how to approach the subjects that were tormenting her—Clorinda's death, the strange sealing of the coffin, whether it was really her fortune he was waiting for, rather than herself. But with his blue eyes laughing down at her, and his lips urgent upon hers, everything seemed to fade into insignificance. She could not believe that he was anything but sincere in his love.

She decided to put all the secrets of Fallows out of her thoughts and simply enjoy his presence. After all, perhaps nothing else of a disturbing nature would happen, and whoever was responsible would stop their foolishness

But the very next morning, her peace of mind was jolted once again. Rupert had some business with the bailiff to see to, regarding his visit to York, and Kitty decided to go riding. She changed into her habit and went out into the balmy morning.

She went to the stables where Starlight, ready saddled, was waiting, and climbed the shallow steps to the mounting block.

The mare seemed unusually restless beneath her, and Kitty took a slightly firmer grasp of the reins as they made their way out on to the open moorland. She drew in her breath at the beauty of it, the moors undulating to the misty horizon, and the wide sky above, the breeze stirring her hair beneath her hat.

With a little sigh of pleasure, Kitty urged Starlight forward, but instead of responding to her heels, Starlight reared, and Kitty was thrown headlong, to land with a thump on the heath. Her head struck a rock half-hidden in the heather, and blackness descended over her.

She returned to consciousness to find that someone was patting her hands and holding a piece of cloth soaked in cold water to her forehead. Bewilderedly, she opened her eyes to see the face of the groom hovering above her.

'My lady? Are you all right, my lady?'

74

'I—think so,' she whispered.

'What happened? Starlight came back with an empty saddle, so I came to look for you,' the groom told her. 'You couldn't have gone far, I knew. What was it? Did something startle the mare? A rabbit?'

'No, I—' Kitty lifted a hand and rubbed her eyes. Her head was aching. 'Nothing startled her. She just reared and threw me, I don't know why.'

The groom was a middle-aged man with a weather-beaten face. As he assisted her to sit up, his expression was grave.

'Starlight was Lady Clorinda's mount, my lady.'

'I know,' Kitty said, her senses beginning to return to her. 'But she behaved perfectly when I rode with Miss Meade.'

He shook his head. 'Happen she knew it wasn't Lady Clorinda who was riding her.'

Kitty began to frame a scornful retort, then she stopped herself, and her pulse pounded. Was the shade of Clorinda resentful that a new mistress was riding her horse in her place? Was this yet another of the strange tricks that were being played upon her? Or was it just coincidence that a gentle animal should suddenly behave in such a wild fashion?

As the groom helped her to her feet, and half-carried her back to the house she found that all her doubts and suspicions were buzzing in her head once again.

75

Rupert was horrified when the groom delivered Kitty, who was still dazed from her fall, and insisted that she lay down and that the doctor should be called, although Kitty tried to protest that apart from an aching head, she was perfectly all right.

When Edward Parsons arrived, he confirmed that she had no injuries beyond a bruise on her head and a few scratches and bruises on the rest of her body.

'A day's rest, and you'll feel fine, Lady Katherine,' He told her.

'But you must never go out riding alone again,' Rupert told her firmly. 'You must have someone with you. If this had happened in some remote place, if you'd been lying on the moor somewhere, I dread to think what might have happened to you.'

After the doctor had gone, leaving instructions that Kitty was to try to sleep for a while, she managed to persuade Rupert to leave her on the sofa in the drawing-room, with the curtains half-closed to shut out the light of the summer day, but she did not even attempt to sleep. She wanted to think.

Lying there, in the dim light, she went over all the events that had taken place since she arrived at Fallows. Had Rupert given her any cause to suspect that he might be marrying her for her money, or trying to harm her? As she lay there, she came to the conclusion that all he had said about loving her was true, and that he genuinely cared very much. No, she decided, it was not Rupert who was playing these foolish jests on her. He knew nothing about them.

Kitty's mind wound on, and she realised that the pranks and mysteries appeared to have a purpose. And that purpose was to sow doubt in her mind about Rupert, and to cause them to part. Someone wanted to come between them—though who and for what reason she did not know. But one thing she decided to do, as soon as possible, was to tell Rupert everything. She would keep no more secrets from him. And, her decision made, she slept at last, to wake refreshed when he came tip-toeing in to see whether she wanted anything to eat or drink.

She felt almost herself again as they ate the tea that Mrs Potter had prepared, toast, muffins dripping with butter, home-made jam, cakes, and a cup of tea that brought the colour back to Kitty's cheeks.

Rupert was loving and considerate, and when tea was over, she said, taking her courage in both hands, 'Rupert, I'd like to talk to you.'

'Of course, darling. We'll talk all evening if you feel well enough,' he replied, taking her hand, but she pulled it from his grasp, gently, but insistently.

'No, Rupert, this is very important. I feel perfectly well now, and what I have to say is something that you might find difficult to believe, but I want you to listen carefully. I think we had better go out into the garden and walk.' She glanced round the drawing-room. 'In a house, even the walls have ears.'

He did not laugh, as she had thought he might. Instead he asked practically, 'Shall you be warm enough in just that thin gown, darling?' For she had changed out of her torn habit after the doctor had examined her into a house-dress of pale blue muslin.

'Yes, I think so,' Kitty said, and led the way through the glass doors into the walled garden. Rupert followed, looking taller and sterner than she could ever remember him, a frown on his dark face as she walked down the path ahead of him.

She sat down in the little summerhouse where roses tumbled in a fragrant mass, filling the air with scent, and Rupert seated himself beside her.

'Well, darling?' he said. 'I am ready to listen.'

Kitty took a deep breath, and then began, steadily, 'Rupert, first of all, I want to tell you that I am neither fanciful or nor of an over-imaginative turn of mind. But I have discovered since I arrived here that there

78

is, for want of a better word, some sort of adversary who has singled me out as a victim. It may even be you, and if it is, I am putting myself into danger by telling you this, but I love you so much that I would rather meet danger, or even death at your hands than believe the things that have been suggested to me, and become disillusioned about my feelings towards you.'

'Danger? Death?' Rupert echoed, tensely. 'Do you realise what you are saying, love? Do you seriously think I would ever harm you?'

'No, deep down inside, I don't believe you would, but I am surrounded by secrets and mysteries, and I cannot take anyone for granted, not even you,'

Kitty said. 'But please let me continue, Rupert. It all began when the coach was stopped and the strange gipsy woman warned me to beware of Clorinda, on the evening I arrived here. Since then, I have been the subject of pranks—jokes—call them what you will, which I have come to think are intended to part us.

'I told you I had been through the Monk's Door, and nobody believed me, but I swear to you that I did not dream these things. They were engineered by my faceless adversary, and I can describe to you exactly what lies behind the Monk's Door and up the stairs. But there is more to it than that. There have been other, small things . . .'

79

She proceeded to tell him about the perfume, the bottle which had mysteriously appeared among her own, Clorinda's gloves.

'While you were away, nothing of any significance occurred,' she added. 'But this morning, Starlight throwing me was not an accident. Oh, I'm not quite a fool, Rupert. It would have been easy for someone to slip a prickly burr or some similar irritant beneath Starlight's saddle, so that she would behave wildly, perhaps cause me to have a serious accident. And then for hints to be dropped that I had been thrown because I was not Clorinda, but was riding Clorinda's mount.'

She waited for him to comment but he said nothing, only folded his arms, his face in shadow, so that she could not see his expression.

'There is more,' she went on. 'When Edward Parsons called to visit me, I asked him about Clorinda, and he told me that she too had seen and heard things which appeared to be the results of fancies and imagination—he said she was unbalanced. But I do not believe she was. I believe she was subjected, as I am, to this mysterious form of persecution, but that she did not know how to deal with it, and was too young to able to decide that some human agency was behind it, rather than the supernatural. I admit I was shaken to discover that she too had been a victim, and I confided in Rosalind, hoping she would be able to formulate some suggestion as to who was responsible.'

'You told Rosalind?' he said quietly, and she nodded.

'Yes.'

'And what did she say?' he asked in the same, calm voice.

'Her suggestion was that you had married Clorinda, and were planning to marry me, because you wanted our fortunes, and that it must be you who was responsible for the strange happenings,' Kitty told him bluntly. 'The only other thing she could think of was that perhaps Clorinda did not die, but was still alive, and it was she who was playing tricks upon me—a suggestion that I find quite preposterous, though I have the doctor's word that apart from yourself, Mrs Potter and the physician who was staying here from London, there was no one else with Clorinda when she died, and that her coffin was sealed immediately.

'Rosalind suggested that perhaps you were all conspirators, and that it was an empty coffin which was buried in the vault. I don't know, Rupert. But I am only concerned with my relationship with you. Someone, or something, is trying to make us quarrel, to doubt each other to part us—and I do not want that to happen.'

* * *

There was a silence in the peaceful twilit garden, with the last of the sun ruddy on the chimneys of Fallows as it lay before them. Then Rupert spoke.

'My Kitty, you are indeed sane and sensible, as well as beautiful, and you are wise with a wisdom I respect.' He leaned forward so that she could see his face, which was troubled, and, lifting her hand to his lips, he kissed it reverently.

'I will swear to you, on a stack of Bibles if you wish, that I married Clorinda to please my father, but I never harmed a hair of her head. And I want to marry you because I love you. Your money does not enter into it. I love you more than anything else in the world, and I could never, ever, do anything to hurt you. Will you accept my word that I am innocent of any plan, or secret, which is intended to bring you distress?'

Kitty felt a surge of deep relief. 'Yes, my darling. I believe you,' she said, taking his hand in both her own. 'But do you believe me? I know my story must sound quite fantastic.'

'Not so fantastic as you think,' was Rupert's surprising answer, as he leaned towards her. 'I confess that I did not at first think any more of your tales of the Monk's Door than that they were bad dreams, but now that you have found out about Clorinda, Kitty, I will tell you something. I did not admit it to anyone, but for some time before her death, I had begun to suspect that there was more to her tales of strange happenings than met the eye.

'I could not believe, however, that such things could take place beneath my roof without my being aware of the culprit—and Clorinda was very different from yourself much more hysterical and incoherent in what she said, and what she described. I could not quite disregard Edward's opinion that her mind was unbalanced, either. And so, to my eternal shame, I let her go to an unhallowed death still believing I thought her insane.'

Forgetting Kitty for the moment, he was overcome with grief, and hid his face in his hands.

She touched his hair gently. 'You must not blame yourself, Rupert. I have said that it is a fantastic story. But now, the same thing is happening to me, and I must have your advice. What should I do? Where shall I turn? Clorinda is gone, and I need you to help me before it is too late—as it was for her.'

He looked up and grasped her in his arms, holding her so tightly against his chest that she could hardly breathe.

'We'll fight this together, love,' he vowed grimly, still holding her. 'I'll not be parted from you, and I'll not lose you too, as I lost that poor innocent girl. I believe everything you tell me. We must make a plan of our own to overcome whoever is responsible for driving

Clorinda to her death and for frightening you.'

'A plan? What sort of plan?' Kitty asked, as he loosened his hold a little, and he pondered for a few moments, his eyes narrowed.

'Whatever you see—or hear—or whatever happens, behave as Clorinda did,' he told her. 'Shriek—scream—ring for Lucy. And I will come rushing to you and pretend to think you are being fanciful. We may even argue about it, and you may weep, as though we are on the point of our relationship breaking up. I will act as though I have no patience with you, and you will accuse me of indifference and heartlessness. But we shall know that it is only for the sake of our adversary, who appears to be well-informed as to our reactions.'

'I suspect Mrs Potter is involved in some way,' Kitty told him, and he nodded.

'The same thought had come to me, for Clorinda actually accused her of being her enemy, and now that we believe Clorinda's story, we must not dismiss what she said lightly. But if I were to question Mrs Potter, she would merely deny all knowledge of such happenings. If I were to dismiss her, we do not know how our mysterious adversary would react. There may be others involved in the house—and we do not want to give away the fact that we are aware that there is a plot to frighten and harm you, nor that we are simply pretending that our relationship is breaking up. Everyone must believe you are trying my patience, and that I do not accept your versions of what you see or hear.

'But darling—' he took both her hands again, holding them tightly—'each time anything occurs, you and I will discuss it afterwards, and try to discover what it tells us about our enemy—for if anyone is trying to part us, then they are my enemy as well as yours. Or, if you are in danger or in need of help, come to me straight away—or send Lucy to me. You trust Lucy?'

Kitty nodded. 'Yes, I think I can trust Lucy. She is innocent of intrigue. Shall I tell her of our plot?'

He frowned.

'Perhaps not yet. We may require her assistance later, but the fewer people who are aware that we are seeking out a maniac—for the person responsible must be insane, and he or she has already caused one death– the better.'

'I feel much braver, knowing you are with me in this, Rupert. You have the heart of a lion, and I am proud that you consented to marry me.'

Relief and gratitude at his understanding swept over Kitty, and she gave herself to the savouring of the sweet moments with his arms around her and his lips on hers. Together they would overcome whatever evil lay hidden in the rooms and corridors of Fallows. It would be a happy place for their children to grow up in, she vowed herself. They would sweep away the cobwebs and secrets once and for all time.

*   *   *

Kitty went to her room that night wondering slightly apprehensively whether anything untoward would occur, but, once again, her sleep was undisturbed, and the next day, she said to Rupert that perhaps whoever was playing the foolish pranks on her had decided to stop their activities.

He did not altogether agree. 'It may be that you are being lulled into a sense of false security, darling. Then, when you suspect it least our enemy will strike. So do not give up your vigilance. Be on your guard.'

But Kitty, flushed and happy after a glorious day in the company of her dearest Rupert, was completely unaware as she relaxed on the day-bed at the foot of her four-poster before dressing for dinner that evening. They had spent the afternoon walking over the moors, and the fresh air and sunlight had tired her so that she was content to follow Rupert's instructions to rest for half an hour before Lucy came up with her hot water.

She lay, watching the last of the afternoon sun slanting across the room and reflecting from the surface of the long mirror, with golden motes dancing in the shafts of light. She was completely happy, and blissfully at ease.

Then, in the mirror, she saw the door open behind her, and said drowsily, 'Is that you, Lucy?'

But no pert footsteps came pattering in and her only answer was a deep silence. Kitty closed her eyes. She must tell Rupert that her door required a firmer catch, so that it would not open on its own. But when she opened her eyes again, the door, reflected in the mirror, was wide, and in the dimness of the corridor beyond, as though formed from the sunbeams on the mirror glass, a figure stood, still as a statue.

Kitty froze, and her heart seemed to leap to her throat so that her hand went involuntarily to her breast in order to still its pounding. As though mesmerised, she gazed into the mirror, at the long copper hair that fell to the girls' waist and the soft folds of her white gown. The face was a blur, but Kitty knew who she was. She struggled to sit up, and spun round to the doorway.

The corridor beyond was empty.

Trembling all over, Kitty rose to her feet and ventured hesitantly to the door, but when she dared to peep through, there was only the bare corridor, with no sign that anyone had stood there. She leaned against the doorframe, while her fright struggled with commonsense to tell her that it was not, could not have been Clorinda who had stood so quietly outside her door. It was just as Rupert had predicted, the enemy had struck when she was least suspecting.

The thought of Rupert reminded her of their plan, and quickly, she rang the bell wildly, until Lucy came running.

'Lucy—Lucy—I have just seen a ghost,' Kitty gasped, grasping the other girl's arm as though terribly frightened. 'Fetch the master, quickly.'

She sank down on to the bed while Lucy ran off along the corridor, and within a few moments, Rupert, who had been in the process of tying his cravat in preparation for going down to dinner, came striding into the room, followed by Mrs Potter. Kitty held out her arms and he pulled her close.

'My love, what is it? What has upset you so?'

'I saw a ghost,' Kitty told him, trying to make her voice tremble. 'It was Clorinda. She came and stood outside my door and I saw her in the mirror.

Rupert exchanged an anxious glance with Mrs Potter, while his hands smoothed Kitty's hair.

'Darling, there are no such things as ghosts,' he said a trifle brusquely. 'What you saw was just your imagination, when you were only half awake.'

'I did see her, I tell you, dressed as she is in the portrait in the Winter Parlour,'

88

Kitty insisted, letting her voice rise. 'It was Clorinda.'

'And what did this ghost do, except stand in the passage outside?' Rupert asked, playing his part at trying to be patient with a hysterical woman.

Kitty shook her head. 'She did nothing. When I turned round, she—she wasn't there. But I did see her—I did!'

'A calming potion, if you please, Mrs Potter,' Rupert ordered, and the housekeeper walked impassively from the room. When she had gone, Rupert whispered in Kitty's ear, 'Well done, love.'

Aloud, for Lucy's benefit, he said soothingly, 'There, there, darling, sit back and in a moment Mrs Potter will bring you something to drink.' He turned to Lucy. 'Did you see any sign that there had been anyone or anything in the corridor when Lady Katherine rang the bell?'

'No, sir,' Lucy said, shaking her head in concern. 'There was nobody.'

'Of course, there would have been nobody, if it was a ghost. Unless Clorinda is still alive,' Kitty said wildly.

'Oh, my lady, she's at peace these two years,' Lucy declared, coming to help Rupert hold Kitty down. 'I truly believe she is at rest.'

Rupert looked long and hard at the maid's distracted expression. 'You love your mistress, don't you Lucy? he asked gently, and she

89

flushed.

'I—yes, sir, she's a real good lady, and I hate to see her upset like this.'

He leaned over to pat her hand. 'Don't worry, Lucy. She will soon be well and herself again, I promise you.'

Lucy kept her head averted from Kitty's fond glance, and they waited in silence until Mrs Potter returned with a cup of cordial.

'Thank you, Mrs Potter,' Rupert said. 'Kindly be so good as to leave the cordial with me. Now you and Lucy may go, and I will settle my fiancée for a short rest until she is calmer. We will postpone dinner for an hour, I think, and by then I hope to have Lady Katherine better. Please inform Cook.'

'Yes, sir,' Mrs Potter said, and she went out, followed by Lucy, who lingered, looking back at Kitty's prone figure on the bed.

Rupert picked up the cordial, and leaned over his beloved saying, 'now, darling, drink this. It will do you the world of good.'

The door shut behind Lucy's departing skirts and Rupert immediately rose and poured the cordial, which was colourless, into the slop-basin on the wash-stand. He came back to Kitty, who had pulled her robe round her more comfortably, shaken back her hair, and sat up.

'Now, love,' Rupert said, as he seated himself beside her. He kept his voice very low. 'You can tell me all about it. But speak quietly.

We do not know who may be listening at the door at any time. You have seen something else?'

'Yes. Someone masquerading as Clorinda,' Kitty told him steadily. 'Rupert, is she really dead?'

CHAPTER EIGHT

Rupert's face twisted with pain.

'Yes, my darling, I swear to you that she is dead. Some time I will tell you more about her death, but even now the memory of that dreadful night haunts me.'

Kitty touched his hand. 'I'm sorry, Rupert. I did not wish to cause you distress, but this means that my first fright over seeing her was simply weakness on my part. It was a living person, I am sure of it, but at least it was not Clorinda herself.'

'No,' Rupert agreed, frowning. 'I do not believe in ghosts or spirits. Exactly what did you see?'

Kitty described to him the image that had appeared to her in the mirror. 'But when I gathered myself together and turned round, she had vanished,' she went on. 'I looked in the corridor, but there was no one there, so she must have hidden herself somewhere. Do you think we would find her if we were to search?'

'I doubt it,' Rupert said, gravely. 'Whoever is doing these things obviously has ways and means of which we are not aware, of appearing to vanish into thin air. Did the figure remind you of anyone?'

Kitty shook her head. 'No, I could not see the face clearly, but the impression was definitely that of Clorinda as she was painted in the portrait downstairs.'

'Naturally,' Rupert pointed out. 'Otherwise you might not have recognised the figure of an unknown woman. Well, this seems to make a change in the tactics of our adversary. I wonder if the intention was simply to frighten you? To make you think you were seeing something supernatural?'

'I can think of no other reason. And I confess, I was frightened at first,' Kitty told him. 'But then I remembered our plan. Oh, Rupert, I'm so glad you believe me, that you don't think I am fanciful, or lying to you.'

He smiled reassuringly, but said. 'I cannot help wondering what the next step will be. I wish I could assure myself that you are in no danger.'

'But the woman, whoever she was, did nothing to harm me. I am certain she is simply trying to frighten me, as poor Clorinda was frightened. Probably the ghost of your mother appeared to her, to make her believe that it was she who was haunting her,' Kitty said, frowning. Then she squared her jaw. 'But it will take more than a few vague glimpses of the supposed ghost of Clorinda to persuade me that I am going mad, Rupert.'

*   *   *

To her surprise and pleasure, Lucy said, as she was putting the finishing touches to Kitty's hair, before she went down to dinner, 'My lady, I don't want to speak out of turn, like, but if I can help you in any way—if you are in, well, difficulty, or want to talk to someone—I know I am only your maid, and I'm not very old, but—I don't like to see you upset.'

'Oh, Lucy dear, what a sweet thing to say,' Kitty told her, moved and touched by the girl's obvious concern. She turned from the mirror to look at Lucy, who was flushed, as though she had committed some error, and smiled kindly as she took her little maid's hand.

'If I need to confide in anyone, you will be the first person I shall turn to,' she said. 'There is just one point, Lucy, that you should know, but I would like you to keep it to yourself. I am sure I can rely on your discretion. Not a word to anyone, not even Mrs Potter or any of the other servants.'

'I can keep my mouth shut, my lady,' Lucy told her, bluntly.

'Well, there are strange things happening in this house, and I want you to know that,

93

however much Sir Rupert and I seem to be drifting part, in reality, we are as close as ever. I could not bear for you to imagine that there was any real ill feeling between us, however oddly you might see us behaving in public.'

Lucy's face cleared. 'I'm right glad of that, ma'am. It was worrying me, that you and he seemed to be getting like—well, like he was with Lady Clorinda.' Then she looked straight into Kitty's eyes, with great seriousness, and said, 'I'll ask no more questions, my lady. You'll tell me what you want me to know. But if there is anything I can do for you, or for the master, you know I'm here.'

'Yes, indeed I do. And, Lucy, thank you, my dear.' Kitty smiled as the little maid bobbed a curtsey. Then she swept from the room to descend for dinner, drawing her face into a petulant expression for Mrs Potter's benefit.

Kitty found it difficult to sleep that night, since the air was humid, and she was worried in case the figure of "Clorinda" might appear again. She had still not managed to get a lock or bolt put on her door, and so, when the great clock at the foot of the stairs struck the hour of two, she was still awake, lying rigid, unable to relax.

After the clock had struck, she heard another sound, and she started up on her pillow, the hair rising on the back of her neck. But after straining her ears for a few seconds, she realised with some relief that the sounds did not come from within the house, but from without, and she had heard them because her window was flung wide to let in the night air. There were stealthy footsteps crossing the paved path outside.

Kitty immediately rose from her bed, and hurried on bare feet to the window, where she held her breath as she peered from behind the shadow of the curtain. There was moonlight, and she saw a figure moving in the direction of the kitchen quarters. Her heart pounded. Was it the mysterious woman who had impersonated Clorinda?

But, no, she saw at a glance that this was a man, though his figure was draped in a long dark cloak. But the pale light glinted on blond hair, and Kitty whispered to herself in astonishment. 'Why, it's Sebastian Meade!'

What on earth was Sebastian doing wandering round the house in the early hours of the morning, she wondered. But even as she watched, she saw another dark shape move from the shadows and the two below her met some distance from her window, and appeared to be conversing in whispers, though she could not hear what they were saying. But yet again, she had recognised the second shape. It was that of the housekeeper, Mrs Potter.

She stood, her head whirling. She and Rupert were convinced that Mrs Potter was in some way connected with their unknown adversary. And now she, Kitty, had witnessed a meeting, obviously arranged, between the housekeeper and Sebastian. Was Sebastian the faceless enemy who wished to part her from Rupert?

Suddenly Kitty recalled the evening when the Meades and the doctor and the Vicar had come for dinner, and Sebastian's warning that he would try to part her from Rupert if he could. Her pulse began to race. Had she unknowingly stumbled on the answer to their mystery? Was it Sebastian who was responsible for somehow arranging the strange events that had happened to her, so that he could have her to himself?

She was convinced that she was right. Of course, Sebastian could not have played the part of Clorinda, but if Mrs Potter was in league with him, some local girl—some friend of Sebastian's, perhaps—might have been persuaded to enact the part, and Mrs Potter could have let her into the house stealthily, and out by the same means.

Kitty debated whether to go straight to Rupert and tell him what she had seen, but the fact that it was the middle of the night, and it would be against the proprieties to creep stealthily into a man's bedroom, even though they were about to be married, held her back. She would tell him tomorrow . . .

When Lucy brought her tea in the morning, she told the girl she wished to hurry and dress so that she could go down to see the master, but Lucy's reply dismayed her.

'The master's gone, my lady. He had an urgent message from one of his tenant farmers who lives on the other side of the moor, and he rode straight after he'd eaten, very early.'

'Oh, dear,' Kitty said, biting her lip, 'I did so want to see him myself.'

'He left you a note, ma'am. It's here on your tray,' Lucy told her, and hastily Kitty unfolded the sealed paper and perused the few words in Rupert's bold handwriting.

Darling.
I have had a request to visit one of my tenant farmers immediately, and it is something I cannot ignore. I shall therefore be gone when you rise, but hope to be back some time this afternoon. Take care of yourself, and remember, I love you. Your Rupert.

Kitty tucked the paper into her bodice, close to her heart. At least he would not be gone for long. She smiled at Lucy, rather ruefully. 'Well, I suppose business must come before pleasure. He will be back later today. I shall sit in the garden and read, to pass the time— it looks as though it is going to be a very hot day.'

After breakfast, which she lingered over, having no reason to hurry now that she could not speak to Rupert, she debated whether to

97

read or to take out her embroidery into the summer-house, and decided on a book. But she had not been sitting there long when the figure of Robbs came at a dignified pace cross the grass.

He bowed slightly, as he informed her, 'Mr. Sebastian Meade has called, my lady. He apologises for the early hour of his call, but says he must speak with you on a matter of extreme importance.'

Sebastian! For a moment, Kitty did not know what to do, then she realised that here was an opportunity to try and unmask her enemy.

'Are you sure he knows that the master is away from home?' she asked Robbs, and he inclined his head.

'Yes, my lady. Mr Meade stated that it was you he wished to speak with in particular.'

'Then you may send him out here to me,' Kitty ordered, thinking that no one would overhear them talking in the garden, and Robbs bowed again, and turned back to the house. Within a few moments, the tall, blond figure of Sebastian came striding across to her, and he bowed in a dashing manner.

'Lady Katherine. How beautiful you look this morning.'

'I believe you have something to say to me?' Kitty said, flushing slightly, but trying to retain her dignity, and he became serious.

'Indeed I have. Lady Katherine Mallory, I

have thought of nothing but you ever since we met. You have haunted all my dreams. I have come to ask you to marry me.'

'Marry you?' Kitty echoed, incredulously. She was too taken aback to utter another word, then she stood up and faced him with her chin in the air.

'Mr Meade, I find your sense of humour rather lacking taste. You know perfectly well that soon I am to be married to Sir Rupert.'

Sebastian seized her hand, and she could not pull it away, for his grip was too strong.

'Katherine, I was never more in earnest in my life. I adore you, I worship you. Does Rupert value you beyond the moon and the stars? To me, you are perfect, I beg you, leave Rupert, break off your engagement and marry me instead.'

Kitty was so bewildered by the turn the conversation had taken that she did not know what to say.

'I love Rupert,' she managed, at last. 'You have no right to come to me with your proposals. I do not love you—I don't even know you—except,' she added, thinking of the previous night, 'that I suspect you are not always above board in your dealings.'

'What makes you say that?' he frowned, his fair brows coming together ominously, and Kitty remembered that perhaps he was her secret enemy. She decided to carry war into the enemy camp.

'I saw you in the garden in the early hours of this morning, behaving in a most furtive fashion,' she said boldly. 'What were you doing, skulking around the house at such an hour?'

'I can tell you that without a qualm,' he replied, taking her other hand so that she was virtually a prisoner. 'I was bribing Mrs Potter to deliver a false message from a far off farm to Rupert, so that he would leave you alone today and I would have the chance to talk with you. I want you very badly Katherine.'

She stared into his green eyes. 'So badly that you would stop at nothing to make me part from Rupert?' she asked slowly, testing her ground.

'Nothing,' he admitted, and Kitty felt certain now that he was the person behind the strange happenings at Fallows. Yet she dared not tell him that she knew of his plot to part her from her beloved. Instead, she changed the subject.

'And what does Rosalind have to say about all this?' she asked challengingly.

He frowned once again. 'Rosalind knows nothing. This affair is between us two.'

'And Mrs Potter, seemingly. It appears that Rupert's trusted housekeeper is not above taking bribes to his disadvantage,' Kitty said scathingly. 'I shall have to tell him of this, naturally, and he will probably dismiss Mrs Potter from his service.'

'You would not do that. You are too kind,

too generous. I have admitted that I bribed her, but it was only because she could see how desperate I was to talk to you, to tell you of my love, that she agreed—most unwillingly—to deliver the false message, he said, appearing distressed.

'And when I say "bribe",' he went on, 'I do not speak of money. It was the wrong word. She took nothing from me. She would agree to nothing, only to give me the chance to speak to you alone, without Rupert's knowledge. And she said that she thought my cause was lost, for you were very much in love with your betrothed. So I beg you, do not blame her for her small part in this matter.'

Kitty did not know whether he spoke the truth or not. 'Have you had any other dealings with Mrs Potter?' she asked, recalling that the housekeeper appeared to be involved in the mysterious events that had taken place, but Sebastian shook his head.

'No, I did not think she would go any further, except to give me this one chance.'

'How can I believe you? How can I know that you have not been to the house before, or bribed other members of the staff to do things for you?' Kitty demanded, and he tightened his grip on her hands.

'I swear I have not. I have tried to forget you, for in spite of my impetuosity on the evening when we came for dinner, I am not a man who would stoop so low that I would steal

101

my best friend's bride from him without a great deal of heart-searching. But Katherine—' his voice grew husky—'I love you so much my darling. I cannot exist without you. I have a right to fight for my happiness.'

'And what of Rupert's happiness? How do you think he would feel if he were to be jilted almost on the very eve of his wedding?' Kitty said sharply. 'Not to mention my own feelings in the matter. I am not an object to be passed from one person's hands to another. I too have emotions. I am sorry, Sebastian, truly sorry, but I love Rupert and I do not love you.'

'You would come to love me, in time,' he said, and his arms were round her, his lips on her hair. To her dismay, Kitty felt the magnetism of his personality, and the lure of his body, making her weak, but resolutely, she pulled herself from his grasp, and slapped his face with all the strength she could muster.

'How dare you!' she panted, her outrage all the stronger because she had so nearly given way to his charm.'

'I will dare anything if only I can win you,' he told her, making no move, but simply standing before her, her palm-print red across his cheek.

'Well, I can assure you once and for all that you will never win me. Good morning, Mr Meade,' Kitty said formally, tapping her foot, and he bowed impassively, and turned. She watched him go back across the garden, and round the side of the house, then sank down on to the seat in the summer house, her knees shaking beneath her.

CHAPTER NINE

Rupert arrived back just after luncheon, his mood black because when he had reached the farm, he had, of course, discovered that he had been summoned on a false errand.

As he strode into the hall, he shouted for Mrs Potter, and when she came, he demanded furiously, 'Where did you get that note for me? It was a fake.'

'I know nothing about it, sir, except that it was brought very early by a travelling gipsy, who happened to be coming this way, and told me a farmer had given it to him and asked him to bring it here,' Mrs Potter stated calmly, and Kitty, who was standing in the doorway of the library, drew a breath at such duplicity, and stepped forward, her eyes flashing.

'Forgive me for contradicting you, Mrs Potter, but that is a lie,' she declared sharply. 'I happen to know that the note was given to you by Mr Sebastian Meade, with the specific intention of removing Sir Rupert from the house so that Mr Meade could call on me this morning with infamous proposals of marriage. I must also add that you need not bother to deny it, for I saw you in the garden in the moonlight at two o'clock last night holding some sort of clandestine meeting with Mr Meade.'

Rupert's gaze swivelled from Kitty to the housekeeper, incredulously. 'Is this true?' he asked, visibly shaken.

Mrs Potter inclined her head. 'Yes, sir. I do not deny it. But I thought that perhaps Lady Katherine might not wish you to know of her encounter with Mr Meade this morning, and I was attempting to protect her.'

'Why should I not tell Sir Rupert that Mr Meade had called?' Kitty asked, frowning, and Mrs Potter pursed her lips and gave a slight shake of her head behind Rupert's averted face. She said nothing.

'Well?' Kitty demanded haughtily. 'I insist upon an answer.'

The housekeeper seemed reluctant to reply, then she said tonelessly, 'Anyone looking out of the windows when you were with Mr Meade in the garden this morning would have seen you in his arms, my lady.'

'In his arms?' Rupert thundered, his fists clenching. 'And what do you mean by that, may I ask?'

'What I say, sir.' The housekeeper's voice was flat. 'Mr Meade was embracing Lady Katherine.'

Rupert turned to Kitty, his eyes bluer than ever with anger. 'Is it true?' he hissed.

104

Kitty was breathing quickly. Something had gone horribly wrong. Then suddenly, she realised that this was another of the traps laid to part her and Rupert, and she lifted her chin.

'If the same people who were spending their time spying on me instead of getting on with their work had seen Mr Meade put his arms around me, they should also have seen that I managed to pull myself free and slap him on the face,' she said calmly. 'Mrs Potter, you are excused. Rupert, please come with me into the library.'

Her tone was so imperious that neither of them argued with her. Mrs Potter bobbed a curtsey and turned away, while Rupert, still smouldering, followed Kitty into the library, where she shut the door firmly behind them.

'Before you say anything, darling Rupert, just listen to me for a moment,' Kitty continued in a low, intense voice. 'You are angry with me, really angry, but this is what he wants. I have found out who our enemy is—Sebastian Meade! I was going to tell you this morning, but you had gone before I came down. And now his latest trick has succeeded. He has caused us, or almost caused us to quarrel.

'But it isn't going to work. I won't let it. Sit down, and I will tell you all that happened this morning. He actually had the audacity to tell me himself that he would stop at nothing in order to part us. And Mrs Potter is on his side.

105

I can see it all now. But at least listen to me before you accuse me of being unfaithful to you.'

In swift words, she told him of the meeting between Sebastian and Mrs Potter that she had witnessed during the night, and of Sebastian's visit that morning, and what he had said. Rupert's face remained dark, but it was with fury at Sebastian, not anger at Kitty, and at the end of her story, he reached out and gripped her hand.

'The scoundrel! Friend? If he is my friend, I dare not imagine what my enemies are like. My darling, I should have known better than to doubt you even for a moment, And Mrs Potter is a viper in the house. I shall dismiss her—no, I insist. She shall go, whatever reaction her dismissal evokes from Sebastian and whoever else is involved in his dirty work.'

'You think I'm right, then?' Kitty asked. 'You agree with me that it must be Sebastian who is our enemy?'

'It would certainly appear so—although why he has resorted to childish tricks, and why he played such tricks upon Clorinda, if, indeed, he was responsible, I do not know,' Rupert said slowly.

He sat deep in thought for a moment, then went on, 'I think we must keep an open mind here, my darling. Apart from his love for you, and his desire to possess you himself, he seems to me to have no motive for all these

106

odd things that have happened—not for what happened to Clorinda.'

'Perhaps Clorinda really did see and hear things that were not there,' Kitty suggested, but her tone was unconvincing, and Rupert pressed her hand.

'We will certainly keep Sebastian in mind as a possible suspect, but our enemy must still remain faceless. So stay on your guard, sweet. Be wary. Anything may happen.' he set his finely-chiselled lips firmly. 'Especially since I am now going to dismiss Mrs Potter.'

'I'm afraid of what may happen if you do,' Kitty said, uneasily.

'But she must go. We now have evidence that she acting with others against my interests. Pull the bell, darling, and I will have her summoned.'

When Mrs Potter came, she stood in her customary posture, with her hands folded, and asked calmly, 'Is it some luncheon you require, sir? I have warned Cook that you will probably be hungry after your ride.'

'No, it is far more serious than that,' Rupert said sternly. He stood on the hearth-rug, facing her. 'Mrs Potter, I am sorry to have to tell you that I no longer trust you. You have been behaving in a manner I find most unseemly. Though it grieves me to do this after your years of service here, I am afraid I must now tell you that you are dismissed from my employ.'

107

The housekeeper's face crumpled. For a moment, she looked like an old woman. Then she drew herself up.

'I understand, sir,' she said without emotion. 'When do you wish me to leave?'

'As soon as it is convenient for you,' Rupert said. 'You will be given three months' salary, and I will naturally supply you with a reference which I am sure will satisfy any future employer. You may put the story about that it is you who have decided to leave Fallows, not that I have dismissed you, if you wish. I do not wish to blacken your character.'

'You are very kind, sir,' Mrs Potter replied, looking at him with her pale eyes, which gave nothing away. 'I will leave tomorrow.'

'Thank you, Mrs Potter. That is all. And now I would be grateful for the luncheon you mentioned,' Rupert said formally.

'It will be ready in ten minutes, sir,' she told him, and without another word, she turned and left the room, leaving Rupert and Kitty exchanging apprehensive glances.

*　　　*　　　*

Kitty was uneasy for the rest of that day, though she did not quite know why. She felt as though, with the dismissal of Mrs Potter, her adversary would somehow be provoked into action, and she could not help wondering just what that action would be. Her fears were not

108

diminished by the fact that Lucy told her, as she dressed for dinner, that the housekeeper had gone out in the afternoon on some errand of her own, and had not long since returned.

Had Mrs Potter been to tell Sebastian about her dismissal? Was Sebastian really her enemy? Or, if he was not, who had Mrs Potter gone to see, and why? Kitty was uneasy all though dinner and, though Rupert tried to calm her as they sat in the drawing-room afterwards, by talking about their wedding, she eventually retired to bed in a tense and anxious frame of mind.

It was impossible to sleep, she thought, but to her amazement, she fell asleep almost as soon as her head touched the pillow, and no evil dreams disturbed her slumbers. However, she woke suddenly in the early hours of the morning, with her throat dry and her body rigid with fright, and immediately jerked upright on her elbow, looking round in the pale moonlight for the cause of her alarm.

A board creaked outside her door, and she realised that it was this same sound that had awakened her. Someone was standing, or moving about, outside her door. She waited, frozen, for the door to open, but instead, a soft voice whispered, as though from nowhere, 'Katherine! Katherine!'

'Who is it?' she asked, through stiff lips.

'Clorinda,' the voice mourned.

Kitty was seized with terror for a few

moments, then she recollected that she did not believe Clorinda was still alive, she had been at peace these two years. The thought compelled her to act quickly. She rose from her bed, threw on a robe, and determined to discover once and for all who was playing foolish pranks upon her. With steps that she tried to make steady, she went to the door, and threw it open.

In the pale dimness of the moonlit corridor, the figure of a woman stood some six feet away, in the same long white gown, with the coppery hair loose, that she had seen before. Her eyes were dark pits in her blank face, her mouth a gash of blackness. Kitty almost screamed, but instead, she stood her ground, and held her head high.

'You are not Clorinda. She is dead,' she declared flatly. 'Who are you, and what do you want?'

'Come, come with me,' whispered the shadow, and lifted a beckoning hand. She seemed to drift off in the direction of the Monk's Door, and resolutely, Kitty followed. This time she was not afraid, but determined to uncover the mystery once and for all. And she told herself that the figure before her was no ghost, for she had heard the boards of the corridor creak beneath her feet.

The Monk's Door stood open, and the figure of the false Clorinda was halfway up the stairs, as Kitty followed. It was almost pitch dark, yet there was light somewhere, coming from above, and when Kitty reached the landing, she saw that one of the locked doors was also open, and a lamp burned within. Someone was standing beside the lamp, which stood on a table, part of the meagre furnishings of the room, that looked as though it had not been cleaned for years, and when she saw the woman, Kitty caught her breath.

'Mrs Potter! What are you doing here?' She turned to the woman who was disguised as Clorinda, her head high. 'I demand an explanation.'

'And you shall have one, dear Kitty,' said a familiar voice, and the woman reached up and removed the coppery wig, revealing her own bright hair. It was Rosalind Meade. Kitty felt her senses swirling.

'Rosalind!' she said involuntarily. 'What are you doing here? And Mrs Potter? And why have you been playing at being Clorinda?'

Rosalind spoke quickly. 'There is much you should know, Kitty darling, but we have little time. Even now your enemy is plotting your destruction.'

'My enemy? You mean Sebastian?' Kitty demanded, and Rosalind shook her head.

'Sebastian has nothing to do with your danger. You must prepare yourself for a shock, Kitty. Mrs Potter told me this afternoon that she has been dismissed, and if you but knew it, she has been watching over you, trying to protect you from your real enemy. Rupert.'

'Rupert?' Kitty echoed incredulously.

'No, no—you are wrong. Rupert has been helping me to hunt down our adversary.'

'It is all pretence, all lies, darling,' Rosalind said urgently. 'It is he who has been responsible for the tricks that have been played on you, just as I thought. Mrs Potter has been watching over you as best she could, and I have been coming, disguised as Clorinda, to do my part. Rupert did indeed want to marry you for your money, and now he plans to marry you before the arranged date, by force and in secret. Then he will dispose of you.'

'I can't believe it!' whispered Kitty, white-faced.

'It's true. Look, he did the same with Clorinda, and that is why I have summoned you tonight. I have found proof that he was Clorinda's killer, Rosalind said inexorably. 'Come, we must all go. The groom, who has also been my ally is watching over you, has horses ready saddled. We must go at once, before it is too late.'

'Go where?' Kitty demanded, hardly able to grasp what the other girl was saying.

'To the Chasm. There I'll show you the proof of Rupert's guilt.'

Kitty was unable to say more, as Mrs Potter flung a dark cloak that she carried round her shoulders, and opened a second door that

112

led from the room. Kitty was hustled down another flight of stairs, and out through a small and very old doorway.

'So this is how you came and went,' she managed to say to Rosalind, who nodded impatiently.

'Yes, but that doesn't matter now. Come. The horses are in the yard.'

They hurried through the balmy, moonlit night, to where the groom was waiting, holding three saddled horses, and Kitty, feeling as though she must be dreaming, clambered up on to the back of one of them, while Rosalind and Mrs Potter mounted the others.

Then Rosalind called softly, 'Follow me!'

So, clinging to her side-saddle, Kitty was off, the three of them moving in a tight little group, the night breeze lifting her unbound hair and making it stream behind her.

Kitty felt more and more as though she was in some sort of nightmare, as they rode through the night. Rupert her enemy? Sebastian innocent? Mrs Potter and Rosalind doing their best to protect her? It couldn't be true! Somehow, it couldn't be real.

'What is this proof that is at the Chasm, that Rupert killed Clorinda?' she cried to Rosalind, as they rode across the heather, the moonlight turning everything into an unreal landscape, and Rosalind's answer came back on the wind.

'You will see, when we arrive there.'

'I don't want to come! You can tell me

113

without taking me there I am going to return home,' Kitty cried, and tried to stop her horse and turn round, but

Mrs Potter and Rosalind closed in on her, one on each side, and they came to a standstill.

'You must come, darling,' Rosalind told her, and Kitty could see her eyes flashing. She seemed to be angry. 'I won't let you go now.'

'Let me go? I am not a prisoner,' Kitty declared, her spirit roused, and Rosalind smiled.

When she smiled, the awful truth broke upon Kitty at last, for Rosalind's smile was that of a mad-woman, leering with triumph, and she laughed, the same fiend-like laugh that the young woman had heard before, at the foot of the Monk's Stairs. Panic swept over her.

'It isn't Rupert who is my enemy—it's you!' Kitty gasped.

Rosalind threw back her head and laughed all the more. 'I told you she would not be easy prey, Mrs Potter. She has spirit, this one. She is not a timid little mouse like Clorinda.

'Let's get to the Chasm and get it over with,' Mrs Potter muttered, uneasily, and Rosalind took the reins of Kitty's horse from her, and urged the beast onwards with her own.

As Kitty was flung up and down on the saddle, her mind was racing. She didn't understand Rosalind's motive but she must subdue her fear in order to formulate a plan by which she could outwit the mad woman she now knew her to be.

CHAPTER TEN

They had almost reached the Chasm, and
Kitty decided quickly that, from various
things she had read and heard, it was always
wise to humour a mad person, and play along
with them, Rosalind must also have killed
Clorinda in some mysterious fashion, she must
remember that, and no doubt she intended to
kill her too. But a person who had killed was
always vain, they liked to boast about their
wicked deeds. She must try to play for time,
until she could see some way in which she
might escape, and perhaps run for shelter
among the rocks near the Chasm, where she
could perhaps be able to evade her captors.

So, when the horses pulled up at the rocks,
and Rosalind bade her dismount, Kitty did
so without question. Rosalind turned to Mrs
Potter. 'She'll fight. I'll need your help.'

But Mrs Potter seemed afraid.

'Clorinda, well, you know how she died,
ma'am. But to do murder in cold blood!'

'You will do as I say!' Rosalind screamed,
shrilly. 'Take her arm, and I will take the
other, and we'll throw her over.'

Kitty's heart leaped in her throat in panic,
and she spoke hastily, trying to stop her voice

115

from trembling.

'It's all right, Rosalind. I promise I'll stay quiet, but before you carry out whatever you have planned for me, you must at least tell me how you came to be so clever. Why, I never suspected you for a moment. You acted the part of a friend wonderfully. At least satisfy my curiosity before—before I have to die. You cannot deny me the answers to my questions.'

Rosalind smiled smugly. 'Yes, it was the same with Clorinda, too. She never suspected it was me who was behind all the odd things that happened to her, and the ghostly appearances of Rupert's mother. But she wasn't like you, Kitty dear, she was timid and frightened. You've been an adversary I can respect, refusing to be frightened. Of course, it made my plan so much more difficult, that I have had to take this way of finishing you off, by throwing you over the Chasm, instead of waiting for you to go mad with fear, and imagine yourself insane.'

'You were so very good at making me doubt my sanity, though,' Kitty said fervently.

Rosalind relaxed and said, 'You can sit down for a moment, if you like, on this stone, while we talk. I admit it gives me pleasure to tell you what a fool you have been. But don't try any trick to escape me. I can't let you go now. You know too much.'

'Oh, I realise that,' Kitty said, with apparent frankness, and she seated herself on the stone, while her hands moved beneath the cover of her dark cloak, seeking, seeking for a stone, a stick, or anything she might use as a weapon. When the time came, she intended to struggle with all her might to save her life and escape. Her fingers closed over two small rocks with jagged edges, and she clutched them to her while she carried on talking to Rosalind.

'So it was you all the time, who played all the tricks on me? How very ingenious you were.'

'Myself and Mrs Potter,' Rosalind smirked. 'Dear Mrs Potter has been my accomplice ever since Rupert married Clorinda. I pay her well, and I have promised her that she will receive even more when I am the mistress of Fallows.'

Kitty stifled the gasp that almost escaped her, and said innocently, 'When you are the mistress of Fallows?'

'Of course. Why do you think I have done all these things? Rupert is mine. I marked him out long since, when we were children, and I have always longed more than anything else in the world to become his wife and the mistress of his home,' Rosalind explained, as though the point should have been obvious even to the most foolish person.

Kitty saw it all as the other woman spoke. The reason why Rupert's bride and bride-to-be had been persecuted; why Rosalind wanted them killed. Jealousy, fierce and possessive, had driven her insane. She would let no obstacle stand in her way to Rupert and Fallows.

'Of course, he does not realise yet that I am going to marry him,' Rosalind continued reflectively. 'He married that simpering wench Clorinda to please his father—but she was easy to deal with. Then I thought he would turn to me, but instead, he went off to London, and came back with you.'

'And the things you told me about his activities while he was in London—about him gambling, and being in debt—they were not true?' Kitty asked, and Rosalind laughed again.

'Of course not. He is boringly honest and upright—but I want him, all the same. It was rather clever of me, though, don't you think? To try to make you doubt him?'

'Oh, yes,' Kitty said fervently. 'In fact, I am certain that when—when I no longer stand in your way, you will be clever enough to win him. And you are so beautiful, so charming, how will he be able to resist you?'

'Yes, I think I might manage it this time,' Rosalind told her with malicious satisfaction. Then she frowned. 'But first I must get rid of you. Now that you know everything, I can carry out my plan. You are to fall over the Chasm, you see, and Mrs Potter will give testimony that she saw you walking through the house in a mad state, but she did not know where you had gone. Then Ned, the groom, who is another of my accomplices—it was he who placed an uncomfortable twig beneath Starlight's saddle, so that the horse threw you, will say that he saw you go to the stables and lead out a horse, ready saddled, and ride off, but he was not in time to stop you.'

She paused, frowning. 'Perhaps it would add greater credence to the presumed suicide if the horse went over the Chasm too. As though you had ridden straight for the edge, you see, and horse and rider had both gone over.'

'I couldn't do that, ma'am,' Mrs Potter put in quickly. She had been wringing her hands and waiting distractedly while Rosalind talked to Kitty, but now she spoke out. 'I don't mind a bit of haunting, and leading somebody on, but to drive an innocent animal over the Chasm— and to murder a lady that's done nothing—as though I was killing a fly, I don't know if I can bring myself to do it.'

'Think of the money!' Rosalind whispered, cajolingly. 'That lovely money!'

In the silence that followed her words, Kitty lifted her head slightly.

Had she heard something? Her heart leapt. She was certain she had heard the far-off sound of hooves.

'No, I can't,' Mrs Potter mumbled finally.

Rosalind turned into a blazing virago. 'Then I will do it myself. Quickly! Now!'

She seized Kitty's arm, and pulled her to her feet, pushing her to the edge of the Chasm, while Kitty fought grimly, hitting out with the stones in her hands. Rosalind was screaming abuse, and Kitty began to scream too.

'Help! Somebody help me! Rupert! Help!'

Rosalind forced her almost to the edge, her strength the strength of madness, and Kitty had almost given up hope, when she suddenly heard a voice, a dearly loved voice.

'Kitty! Kitty, my darling! Hold on! I'm coming!'

Rosalind whirled about, as Rupert slid from the horse he had been riding bare-back, and sprang forward to where the two women were struggling. He snatched Kitty from Rosalind's grasp, and held her to him, while, weak with relief, she sobbed against his chest.

Rosalind turned her fury to the two of them, and began to hit out wildly at Rupert, while he did his best to protect Kitty from her blows.

'You shan't stop me now! Let me have her!' Rosalind screamed shrilly. 'Mrs Potter—come and help me! That is an order!'

The housekeeper came to Rosalind's assistance, and the two of them had half-dragged Rupert and Kitty towards the Chasm when another voice was heard above the melee.

'Ros! Katherine! Katherine, are you all right?'

'Here!' Rupert called tensely, and the figure of Sebastian appeared from behind one of the rocks. Together he and Rupert seized Mrs

Potter, who gave way resignedly, but Rosalind stood on the edge of the Chasm, her long bright hair streaming in the wind, and faced the men defiantly.

'Seb! Why did you come here? You know?'

'I know enough,' Sebastian answered grimly. 'You're mad, Ros. Come here.'

Rosalind turned to Rupert. 'And Kitty knows, so soon you will know all too,' she said. 'Well, I gambled, and I have lost.' She gave a crooked smile. 'There's nothing left for me now. Only one way out.'

'No—'

'Stop!'

The two men started forward, and Kitty raised a hand to her mouth in horror, as Rosalind turned and without another word, threw herself over the Chasm. Her scream echoed on the night air, then faded away into nothing.

The rest of the little group was silent, then Rupert went to Kitty, who was shaking, and put his arm about her, while Sebastian seized Mrs Potter in a rough grasp.

'Come on, you,' he ordered. 'And no attempts to run away.'

'I won't try to run away, sir,' the housekeeper said emotionlessly. 'She's gone— but I'll take whatever must come to me.'

'Oh, Rupert, what a terrible end! That was what she wanted to do to me,' Kitty gulped, as Rupert held her tenderly.

121

'Come, love. It was the way she chose,' he told her, and she nodded slowly.

'Yes. She was mad, Rupert, insane. What sort of life could she have had if she had lived?'

'It's all over, love,' Rupert said gently. 'Come, let's go home.'

*   *   *

In the restful atmosphere of the house on a sweet, warm morning following the horrors of the night, Kitty was relaxing on the sofa in the drawing-room while Rupert, stunned and infinitely relieved that she had come to no serious harm, sat beside her. Every now and then, he would tighten his hold upon her hand and say, 'Thank God! I nearly lost you, my Kitty!'

Upon their return to the house, Sebastian had taken Mrs Potter away to the authorities, and to inform them of Rosalind's death, and Ned the groom had also been picked up and placed in the custody of the nearest magistrate, on Kitty's evidence that he too had been embroiled in Rosalind's schemes.

She had been shattered and exhausted, and Rupert had immediately summoned Edward Parsons, who came promptly, and examined her, treated her bruises and scratches where Rosalind had clawed at her face, and declared that she needed rest.

122

'I won't go to bed, it's daybreak, it's a new day, and I want to be with Rupert,' Kitty told him. 'We have so much to talk about.'

'Very well, then, but you must not stir from the sofa today. I absolutely insist,' the young doctor said, and she smiled.

'I give you my word.'

Rupert had taken Edward to one side, while Kitty ate a light, but nourishing breakfast prepared by Cook, and told him briefly of what had happened. Edward, too, was horrified at the manner of Rosalind's death, but shook his head when informed of her madness.

'To think I never guessed! I chose to believe that Clorinda—and possibly even Kitty—were imagining things! I will never forgive myself.'

Rupert slapped him on the shoulder, reassuringly. 'Don't worry, old man. How were you to know? Kitty is safe, thank the Lord, and our murderess is no more. It is better that she should have gone as she did, for life in an institution was all that awaited her.'

Edward departed, but their visitors had not finished arriving. An hour later, after Kitty had dozed for a little, and Rupert sat quietly beside her, Sebastian came, his face grave. He joined the little group in the drawing-room, and told them that arrangements had been made to recover Rosalind's body, and have it buried, proceedings would be taken against Mrs Potter and Ned after Kitty had been interviewed by the authorities about what had happened.

Kitty leaned forward sympathetically. 'I am so sorry, Sebastian. She was your sister, and I know how you must feel.'

'Sister or not, she tried to murder you in cold blood, and for that I cannot forgive her,' Sebastian declared. He looked up at her. 'You know that I love you, Katherine. But I can see now that your choice is Rupert, and so I will bother you no more. To think that it was Mrs Potter—Mrs Potter of all people, a mad woman's accomplice, whom I chose to confide in, to try to persuade you to marry me. How she must have laughed. The very thing that she and Rosalind wanted to accomplish—to part you and Rupert. And I played right into their hands.'

'It is time we sorted out all these mysteries,' Rupert declared, holding Kitty's hand tightly.

'Yes,' she agreed, 'there are things I simply must know. What happened to make you aware that Rosalind and Mrs Potter had taken me to the Chasm? How did you—and Sebastian—come to my rescue? I had given up all for lost.'

Rupert settled back, and smiled at her. 'For your safety, you owe a great debt to your little maid Lucy,' he told her.

'Lucy?' Kitty echoed bewilderedly.

'Yes. Apparently she was so worried about you that she took to sleeping in the empty storeroom next to your chamber, where she would be able to come to your assistance in the

124

night if there were any disturbances,' Rupert explained.

Kitty gave a radiant smile. 'Dear Lucy! I must thank her at once for her concern and her action. Shall we call her?'

'Certainly. She has been told you are safe, and is greatly relieved. But perhaps the story of what happened in the night would be better told in her own words,' Rupert said. His eyes twinkled. 'It was she who brushed out your hair and washed your face and hands, and changed your torn night attire for the morning gown you are wearing now, when we arrived back. But you were too exhausted then to notice how it was.'

'Please call her,' Kitty said impulsively, and Rupert rose to ring the bell and summoned Lucy.

'Dear Lucy! How good you have been to me. Rupert tells me that it was you who saved me. You must explain all about it.'

'Oh, my lady,' Lucy gasped and, unable to help herself, she ran into Kitty's embrace. The men exchanged tolerant smiles as Lucy wiped away tears of emotion, and Kitty hugged the young girl to her.

'Please, sit here beside me, and tell me what happened,' Kitty said, after a few moments. 'Rupert says you were sleeping in the chamber next to mine, so that you could come to my assistance if necessary.'

'Yes, ma'am, I—I felt I wanted to be near

you,' Lucy said breathlessly. She looked up. 'Did I do wrong?'

'No, no, you showed how very faithful and loyal you are.' Kitty smiled. 'I cannot thank you enough, dear Lucy. But tell us what happened in the night.'

'Well, I was half asleep, like, and I heard steps along the corridor outside, and a voice talking to you, saying it was Clorinda,' Lucy began, clasping her hands. 'Then I heard you open your door and walk up the corridor after—whoever-it-was towards the Monk's Door, So I—well, crept after you.'

'And you weren't afraid? Oh, Lucy dear, how very brave,' Kitty exclaimed.

Lucy grinned. 'Well, I was frightened, no doubt about it, ma'am, but I was more concerned for you. And I followed you up the stairs behind the Monk's Door, and listened on the landing, and heard Miss Rosalind telling you that you were in deadly danger from Sir Rupert, and how he had murdered Lady Clorinda, and that you and Mrs Potter must come with her to the Chasm.

'I was in a right state then, because if Sir Rupert was really your enemy, and was trying to kill you, I didn't know who else to go to for help.' She paused. The others were listening intently. 'Anyway, I remembered you saying that things were really all right between Sir Rupert and you, although they might not look like it, and I remembered what a good master

126

he had always been, and how gently he'd cared for Lady Clorinda when she was alive, and I thought to myself, "Lucy, there's summat wrong here"—so I decided to risk it and go to Sir Rupert and tell him everything.'

'She shook me like a tigress until I woke.' Rupert smiled at the recollection.

'And blurted out how you'd gone to the Chasm with Miss Rosalind and Mrs Potter, and told me what she had overheard, didn't you, Lucy? And then, of course, I knew who our enemy really was, and I dashed on some clothes and hurried down to the stables— didn't bother to saddle a horse—but rode hell for leather to the Chasm.'

'And arrived just as they were about to push me over the edge,' Kitty finished. She put an arm around Lucy, and looked up at Rupert. 'I don't know how to thank you both.'

'Just marry me.' Rupert smiled.

Lucy ventured, 'Just let me serve you, my lady.'

'Of course. You shall be promoted to being my personal companion and maid, and I'll never forget what I owe to you,' Kitty replied, kissing the young girl, who blushed.

'That's all for now, Lucy,' Rupert said gently, and the young girl rose and bobbed a curtsey, before she left the room.

'So it was thanks to Lucy that you were in time to save me, and knew where I had been taken,' Kitty said, and both she and Rupert turned to Sebastian. 'But how did you come to be on the scene? What brought you there? Without you, we might never have been able to fight Rosalind off.'

Sebastian's face was sombre. 'I was up late, and I chanced upon a book hidden away behind some old volumes that we never read,' he explained. 'I opened it, and found it was a sort of diary, in Rosalind's handwriting. I did not know what to make of it at first, but then I realised that she had been keeping a record of the way in which she appeared to have been tormenting Clorinda, trying to make the poor girl doubt her own sanity. I realised as I read that my sister was—obsessed is the right work, I think—with the idea of marrying Rupert and becoming mistress of Fallows. Then there was a brief record of Clorinda's death.'

'Was Rosalind responsible for that?' Kitty could not help asking.

Rupert lowered his head. 'Only indirectly. I promised to tell you, some day, about how Clorinda died, and explain to why her coffin was sealed up so soon,' he said slowly. 'Perhaps that time is now. And Sebastian, too, has a right to know, having come to your rescue, and being Rosalind's brother.'

He hesitated, then went on in a low voice, 'You already know, and now Sebastian knows, that Rosalind resented Clorinda, and tried to make the poor child imagine she was going out of her mind—aided and abetted by Mrs Potter,

128

whom she bribed, and to whom she promised great wealth when she at last became mistress at Fallows. Mrs Potter was greedy. She allowed herself to be manipulated for the sake of the money.'

'But Rosalind was not there when Clorinda died, was she? It must have been Mrs Potter who killed her,' Kitty hazarded.

Rupert shook his head. 'No. Clorinda was very impressionable, and her mind was becoming unbalanced by Rosalind's tricks and false hauntings. When she had her child, it proved to be the last straw for her sanity, for the infant was born dead. And while we were distracted, at the other side of the room—I cannot bear to think of it even now—Clorinda, my poor child, seized a knife, one of the doctors' surgical knives, and cut her own throat.'

'Oh no!' Kitty exclaimed, a chill creeping all over her body.'

'Rosalind has a lot to answer for,' Sebastian stated grimly.

'Clorinda killed herself, and she struck so deeply with the knife, which was razor-sharp, that the physician could not save her,' Rupert said, heavily. 'She bled to death before our eyes. So you can see why we had to have the coffin sealed. It was so that Clorinda could have a decent burial in sacred ground. And to save the scandal. Only we three who were present—the physician, Mrs Potter and myself—knew, apart from the undertaker's man, who had to be told. We all swore a vow of secrecy, the doctor left immediately, and I have never mentioned it to anyone, nor, I think, has the undertaker's man. Mrs Potter, of course, must have told Rosalind, though she pretended not to know the manner of Clorinda's death.'

'It's—horrible. Poor, poor Clorinda,' Kitty cried, her heart going out to the young girl who laughed down from the picture in the Winter parlour, and who had met such a terrible fate. 'And how dreadful for you, Rupert.'

'I still feel that I was to blame,' Rupert said, lifting a hand to his forehead. 'I might have been able to save her, if only I had believed her tales of haunting and spirits.'

'But you were not to know it was all Rosalind's doing,' Sebastian said sharply. 'She was mad, with a terrible cunning madness. I reached that conclusion when I read on in her diary, about the tricks she had played, or caused to be played, upon Katherine, beginning with the strange gipsy's warning even before she arrived at Fallows.'

'So that was Rosalind?' Kitty asked, and he nodded.

'She really enjoyed herself, that was the terrible part. And then—I came to the last entry, made yesterday afternoon. It detailed what she planned to do with Katherine— entice her to the Chasm during the night, and throw her over. I hesitated for only a moment, then I rushed up to her room. She was not there—and I knew that she had gone out on her deadly errand. So I ran for my horse as quickly as I could, and rode to the Chasm.' He shrugged. 'The rest you know.'

'You have been a true friend, Sebastian,' Rupert said.

'You will always be welcome beneath our roof,' Kitty added warmly, as she held out her hand to the man who had loved—and lost—her.

He kissed her hand gently. 'I thank you. I hope your marriage is filled with warmth and happiness, and your children never know the shadows of fear as you have known them.'

Rupert took Kitty into a close embrace, and looked down into her eyes. 'No, all that is over now, gone for ever. The shadows have lifted, and a lifetime of bliss lies before us. We will hear Fallows ringing with merry laughter, and there will be no doubts, no fears, no dark corners anywhere. Am I not right, my Kitty?'

'Oh, yes, Rupert!' she said fervently, as his lips came down on hers.